SNATCHED

MARIAMA K SANGARIE

BALBOA.PRESS

A DIVISION OF HAY HOUSE

Balboa Press books may be ordered through booksellers or by contacting:

Balboa Press
A Division of Hay House
1663 Liberty Drive
Bloomington, IN 47403
www.balboapress.com
844-682-1282

Print information available on the last page.

ISBN: 978-1-9822-5320-2 (sc)
ISBN: 978-1-9822-5321-9 (e)

Balboa Press rev. date: 01/20/2021

MALAYSIA

Brazzaville! A dream-come-true ever since I saw a documentary about it several years ago. Now I am going for real, with my family! The excitement was non-stop, except for my boyfriend Chris and his playful distractions. There I was, trying to be serious about the dream vacation of my life, and Chris distracted me with his shirtless and captivating dance routine to the 90's pop music we were enjoying...alone in my bedroom...a big no-no that could ruin my dream trip if I get caught! But I couldn't help myself. Those six-packs! That beautiful curly hair! That sharp, cutting jawline! I secretly wanted him right then and there...

"I'm going to miss you, Baby," he says to me in that soft, husky voice...while I shoot back, "I will think of you the whole two weeks we are away." Two weeks....that's a long time for my baby to be away." "I know, but it's my Brazzaville dream trip, I said. "But I still hate that you are going," he whined. Then he asks ever so playfully...are you enjoying my little dance show? It's just for you, baby."

I tried not to answer him back, but my eyes said all he needed to know as they followed him around my room. Then, before I knew what hit me, his hands were on my hips, drawing me closer to him. His manly odor filled my nose with his masculine, pungent aroma. I'm sure my eyes were telling him to kiss me. He started teasing my neck with gentle soft kisses, making my heart pound and my knees weaken. I didn't have to say a word. He knew I wanted him. But I wanted him to hear me say it. "I want you," I moaned softly. He slowly drew back until our eyes were locked. "What did you say"? He asked, wanting me to repeat it. "I want you," I repeated. Now…. right now. Are you *sure*, Asia? Do you know what you just said? I'm sure I repeated to him. "I never want to feel like I forced you to want this…to do something you might regret and then hate me for later". "Baby, you're not pushing me to do anything I haven't wanted to do for months!"

He suddenly had a boyish look on his face, like a kid in a candy store with a fistful of money, wanting everything he laid his eyes on. Chris, I promise you, you're not forcing me to do anything I don't want to do of my own choice. The look on his face was like that kid in the store that had been told he could have whatever he wanted. Suddenly our lips were locked together in a kiss so deep it could have been our last day on earth! This kiss was different than every other time we had kissed. It was deeper, more passionate, and hotter than ever! I found myself leaping off the floor, my legs wrapped tightly around him in a very suggestive way, and he slowly backed me onto my bed. Before I knew what happened, I was unclothed, down to next to nothing. I felt naked…*wanted* to feel naked, with our bodies locked together, although I was aware that I still had my bra and panties on, and he still had his boxers.

"Shit!" he yelled. "Asia I—"

"Here," I said, interrupting him by pulling the condom out of my nightstand. His grin was so big that it reached both sides of his face.

"Malaysia Strawberry Johnson, turn that music down right now!"

My mom came barging into my room, yelling. I couldn't help but yell with fear. I was caught red-handed.

"Oh, crap!" I yelled.

"That's right, oh crap!" my mom said.

"My parents are supposed to be out."

"Hi Mrs. Johnson," Chris said.

My mom gave him the most disgusted look I have ever seen her give to someone. Maybe Chris shouldn't have said anything.

"Janiya, what's wrong?" my dad asked.

Chris was scared of my father. His face began to turn a shade of vibrant red as he realized we were in trouble. I would've been scared of my dad, too, if I was Chris, because of how buff he's. My dad is a retired football player, so he's a pretty big guy.

"We trusted you, and this is what you do," my mom said.

My dad started yelling but decided to leave the room before doing something that he'd regret. Chris was so frightened he shook like a leaf when my dad shouted.

"Little boy, you need to go," my mom told Chris in a cold tone.

Chris gave me a peck and said goodbye to my mom. He was about to walk out in his boxer.

"Take your clothes with you," my mom said.

Chris picked up his clothes and left.

"I trusted you," my mom spoke. "What is our number one rule when we are not home?"

"I'm not allowed to have any visitors when you're out, especially Chris," I answered. "But mom, I didn't invite him. He came here unexpectedly,"

"You were the one who invited him inside the house and into your bedroom," I didn't say anything. My boyfriend came over for a surprise visit. He brought me candy and a new teddy bear. My mom was talking, but I couldn't hear her. My mind was clouded with thoughts of Chris. We were so close. I should have locked my door; I wouldn't have been caught, we would've done it, and I could have snuck him out after we were finished.

"Do I make myself clear?!" Her voice spooked me back into reality.

"Yes, ma'am," I said.

"That's exactly why I am going to talk to your dad about canceling our trip,"

My jaw dropped at the thought of my trip getting canceled. "Momma, please! Please! I'm sorry!" I pleaded. "We didn't do anything!" I cried. "I am so sorry, Momma, but please, I really want to go to Brazzaville."

"You should've thought of that before inviting Chris inside,"

"We didn't even do anything."

"Malaysia, you broke the rules! You're grounded Malaysia, and turn down the music," she said. She left and slammed the door.

I finally turned down the music like I was told. I got grounded, and my trip was taken away, but at least she didn't take away my phone. I am profoundly grateful for that. I needed someone to rant to, and I couldn't rant to my best friend Keisha because she and her family are on vacation in Jamaica, and she's not allowed to use her phone during vacations. I called my older sister Maysie who I can also depend on. Maybe she can soothe me and tell me what to do.

"Hi, Maysie."

"Hello, Asia. How are you?"

"I'm a little stressed with the list you gave me for Koko," she spoke.

"You don't need to worry about her list anymore," I said in a disappointed tone.

"Why?"

"Momma and Daddy canceled the trip to Brazzaville."

"Why?" she questioned.

"Because they caught Chris and me in bed together," I said.

Maysie gasped loudly. I could tell she was shocked. In my family, I'm the youngest and the goody-two-shoes. I'm not used to getting in trouble. In fact, I've never been grounded before; this is the first time. I am the one that gets good grades and awards, not drama and trouble.

"Did you guys do anything?" she inquired.

"No, May, we didn't. Momma barged into my room before we had the chance," I told her.

"Have you guys done it before?" No, Maysie, we haven't; I'm still a virgin," I told her. I was getting irritated with all these questions, and it felt like I was on trial. Maysie could tell that I was getting annoyed with her but continued to ask questions.

"Did Daddy say anything or do anything?" "When Momma was yelling, Daddy came to check on us and caught Chris and me in the bed together. He didn't say anything to me or Chris he just yelled and left," I said.

"Oh, oh, that's not good," May said. "Damn Asia, I never thought I would see you get in trouble," Maysie chuckled.

"It's not funny, Maysie,"

"I'm sorry, you're right, it's not funny," she said.

"I understand that I did something wrong, but I've been waiting for this trip all year,"

"Asia, you did break one of the most important rules," she said.

"He surprised me. I didn't want to be rude and send him off,"

"Momma and Daddy are just worried about you," she said.

"Asia, I'm not going to tell you not to have sex or anything because I'll be a hypocrite. But use protection like a condom, and if you need birth control, I'll buy you some," Maysie said. "I just don't want you to go down the same path that I did," she said. Maysie's advice means everything to me because I know what she went through when she was around my age.

"What do I do about Momma and Daddy?"

"I'll talk to Momma for you. But Asia, you need to understand that no parent wants to catch their child doing that," she said. "I got to go, Asia. I'll talk to you later," Maysie said.

Today was so wild and stressful that I had to take a nap.

Yaff, Yaff.' I heard my brown fuzzy, adorable Shih-poo Koko bark from outside my door. I opened the door to let her in. She wagged her tail excitedly at me. I checked my phone. It's time for her walk. My phone is filled with texts and calls from Chris, making sure that I am okay. I decided to call him back to let him know that I am alright.

"Hello, Chris. I'm sorry, but I fell asleep," I said.

"Chris is the shower," A female voice answered. Her voice sounds familiar like I met her before.

"Okay, who is this?" I asked.

"I am hurt that you don't recognize my voice," she said.

"I'm..so-rry."

"There is no need to apologize; it's me, Addy!" I went from confused to pissed off. What is she doing there? "I can't believe Chris didn't tell you," she snickered.

"Tell me what?"

"Addy, what are you doing in my room?" Chris asked.

"I wanted to ask you to borrow your charger," she said.

"What are you doing with my phone?" Chris questioned.

"I am talking to your girlfriend," she said in a tone like Chris asked a silly question.

"Addy give me my phone," Chris demanded.

"Hey, babe," he said to me.

"What's going on, Chris? Why is she at your house?" I interrogated.

"Well...uh. What happened was..." Chris stuttered.

"Just tell her already!" I heard Addy cackling in the back.

"What the hell is going on?"

"Babe, it's nothing going on."

This isn't sitting right with me. Why does he feel the need not to tell me what's going on? "Chris, tell me what's going on!"

"Babe, trust me, it's nothing

"If it's nothing important, it wouldn't matter if you tell me or not."

"Trust me ... babe ... it is nothing," he said nervously.

I hear Addy snickering. "I can't believe you are not going to tell her, and I thought you guys were the perfect match," she spoke.

"Tell me what?" I questioned.

"What's going on, Chris?"

"Just tell her already."

"Stop patronizing me and tell me what the hell is going on, and why the hell is at your house?!"

I could feel her smirk through the phone. I was triggered by Addison Miller, the girl who has been trying to get Chris and me to break up"

There was a long awkward silence, and I wanted to strangle both of them. *What the hell is going on? Is cheating on me?* **AGAIN**! *No, not possible he wouldn't cheat on me again with the same girl. Right?*

"Chris, you're acting suspicious. Are you cheating on me?"

"Babe, it's not what it seems like," he said.

"If it's not what it seems like, why aren't you answering my question?"

"I'm getting really irritated. If you don't answer my questions, I will hang up!!"

"A—"

I didn't feel like talking to him right now, so I hung up the phone.

I feel like shit, all I really want to do is cuss and scream at both of them, but instead, I hung up and kept to myself. I got Koko's collar and strapped it to her body. I need fresh air to think, and taking Koko for a walk is a perfect excuse without violating me being grounded, I think.

Outside, the hot but cool breeze hit me. It felt quite nice. I've been inside all day. I really miss Keisha, she's probably having the time of her life on the Jamaican beaches, and I'm out here in Cali in my feelings. But today altogether is a terrible day. First, I got caught and grounded, then I'm not allowed to go to Brazzaville, and now my boyfriend—I don't know about Chris yet. Koko kept barking at a shadow heading towards us. My legs began to tremble. I tried pulling her away, but then I heard someone calling my name.

"Are you stalking me?" I asked.

"No, of course not," Chris said.

"Then how did you know that I was outside?"

"It's time for Koko to take a daily walk, and also, when you are angry, you usually go outside," he said. I must have looked irritated because Chris said, "You're predictable when you're pissed off."

"Alright, I'm predictable when I'm mad, so what?" I stated nastily.

"So give me a chance to explain, and don't tell me to leave you alone because I am not going to until you give me a chance to defend myself,"

Maybe I'm a little predictable when I'm mad because Chris was right. I was going to tell him to leave me alone.

"Why didn't you answer my questions?" I asked. "What's going on, Chris?"

"Don't get upset, Asia but...uhm...well ... Addy." His word couldn't come out of his mouth, and he began to stutter. "Addy is what, Chris? What's Addy? Spit it out already!" I yelled.

"Addy's staying with me!" he said like he has been holding it for some time. "She's going to stay at my house until her parents come back from a business trip to Japan."

"Really, Chris?! What? Why didn't you tell me?" I inquired.

"I was afraid that you were going to be angry at me."

"I am your girlfriend; I would have understood that you had no control over the situation," I said.

"Be honest; you just didn't want to tell me."

"No, honestly, I did; I didn't want you to get mad at me because Addison is staying at my place; it's really all my parent's fault. I tried to talk them out of it, but they insisted that she stays at my place," he told me.

"Chris, I'm not mad because of that. You clearly can't control who your parents decide to invite inside their home, but what made me infuriated is that you couldn't have let me know that Addison Miller, the same girl you had sex with last year, is staying at your place," I told him. "What is even worse is that you weren't going to tell me if she hadn't brought it up. Don't get me wrong. Her being at your place makes me livid, but if you talked to me about the situation, this argument wouldn't have happened," I told him. "Maybe you just wanted to keep her a secret. Maybe there is something you're not telling," I continued.

"Asia, trust me, I didn't want to keep her a secret; I just didn't know how to tell you; I promise there is nothing going on"

"Trust is something you earn, and I currently don't trust you,"

His eyes widened, and his mouth slowly dropped wide open. He was trying to say something, but it sounded like gibberish.

"You don't... trust me?" his words finally came out.

"No, I don't," I said blankly.

"A relationship without trust is not a relationship at all," he said.

"You're right," I said.

"Are you breaking up with me?" Chris stared at me without blinking.

"Yes, I am," I told him while staring at the ground.

"You're not serious, Asia...look me in the eyes and tell me you want to break up,"

I couldn't look at him in his beautiful eyes that shimmer with shades of brown and emerald, but sometimes the emerald hues overpower and stand in the spotlight.

"Asia, look at me."

"Chris, I just can't, okay,"

"Why can't you" he demanded. I didn't say anything.

"Do you love me?" he asked.

"I do,"

"Then why are you breaking my heart?"

"Chris, I love you, but I refuse to be cheated on twice with the same girl," I told him. "I really don't want another repeat of junior year. I'm too young to be stressing over stuff like this," I told him, and I tried to walk away, but he grabbed my arm. I looked at him in his pleading eyes and gently tugged my arm, and walked away.

"I'm sorry, Asia!" Chris yelled as I walked away slowly.

I didn't want to turn around and see his handsome face because I know seeing his face again will make me regret everything I just said. I came home all gloomy. It's dinner time, but I don't want to eat because I'm not ready for the awkward dinner with my parents. I gave Koko her water and went into my room. Why does the world have to be so complicated? Today started as a great day. Then it turned into a flop. Imagine getting grounded during the summer—it sucks. I felt so bad that I decided to fall asleep. Maybe today was some kind of a surreal dream. I woke up around five in the morning with a growling stomach. I went downstairs to the kitchen, so I could get some food. I saw someone sitting in the dark downstairs. I got so scared I began to tremble.

"Momma, what are you doing up?" I asked.

"Your sister called me," she said, ignoring my question. "Malaysia, I'm glad you and your sister have each other's backs, but I need you to understand that I'm your sister's mother, not the other way around"

I didn't say anything back. I just listened while my stomach growled.

"When your sister explained to me that you were sorry about

breaking our rules and said that you are a good kid. It got me thinking, taking away the trip was a bit much. Then I realized that it would be a waste of money to not go on the trip your father and I already paid for," my mom said.

Oh my god! I can't believe my ears. That's great news.

"Momma, thank you very much; you're the best mom in the *whole* universe!" I exclaimed. I'm so stoked right now. I'm numb.

Asia, we need to talk about the incident that happened and how you can protect yourself". I am not mad at you for wanting to have sex because you're a teenager, and it is understandable. However, there are a lot of diseases that you can catch that are sexually transmitted" my mom said. Oh my goodness, why? Why? Why? Not the birds and the bees talk; it's too early for this awkward conversation.

"Momma, please let's discuss this later; I am too tired to have this conversation." She scanned my face. I thought she was going to yell at me, but instead, she said, you're right. We will talk about this later on.

"After you go and get your shots at the doctor." I hate the doctors; I'm so nervous about today's appointment that I feel like throwing up. The smell of the hospital is what makes me sick. I ate breakfast and went back to sleep.

Around eight am, I woke up and got ready for my doctor's appointment. After looking through my closet, I decided to wear a yellow t-shirt and jeans. Chris kept spamming me with texts and calls-53 calls. He's the type of person that has ambition and hates to give up. I think that's why I am so crazy about him. I really don't know if I did the right thing by breaking up with Chris, but I'm not going to stay and get cheated on again. I heard a knock on my door. It's my mom telling me to go.

My mom and I were not talking, and the radio was turned off, so all I could hear was the car engine and the AC. I tried to doze off, but we reached the hospital before I had the chance. We waited in the waiting room until the doctor called my name. I got a few shots, and I sweated like a horse. My doctor is really sweet, and she even tried to calm me down.

On our way home, I became really hungry, so I asked my mom if we could grab a bite to eat. I think my voice got her fired up. She went completely off on how irresponsible I could be and how I didn't follow one of our main rules. After her yelling and talking on and on, she stopped at a nice restaurant for us to eat. When we exited the car, fans came and piled at us. They really love our family reality show.

"I order you some birth control pills," she told me. I know that you think that you're ready to have sex, which is understandable; however, there are risks to having sex," she told me. "Mom, I know that's why we were going to use a condom," I told her. "Condoms does not always protect you" "You can catch diseases such as STDs from your partner or even get pregnant while using a condom" "I know that I can't stop you from having sex, knowing you if you want to do something you will stop at nothing to do it. However, I want you to be protected while you do it. I ordered you birth control because I want you to be extra cautious in case there is a day someone forgets to bring a condom," She told me. I don't want any grandkids from you right now. I am way too young," Momma Joked. "Asia, I want you to talk to your dad. You guys need to have a conversation. I know your conversation is probably going to be more awkward with him than it is with me."

"I will try, I promise," I said.

I know she is right about me talking to my dad, but I really don't know how to approach my dad right now. We ate our food, and our lunch was really lovely.

Later on, today, I tried to talk to my dad, but he wouldn't even look in my direction. He refused to sit with me, so while my mom and I ate in the dining room, he ate his dinner in his man cave. I might deserve this, but I am a human being too. I don't like being ignored and especially when I make an effort to have an important conversation.

My ex kept calling and texting me. I know that I was the one who dumped him, but I really miss him. I just want to be wrapped in his arms. I need to be strong. We broke up not because I don't love him because I fear being hurt again. I need to think about good things. I only have one more day before we go to Africa. Koko was whining at my door for me to let her in. She came and laid next to me. I'm really going to miss my baby. She's really the best, and she's also a blessing.

I was playing with Koko when I received a phone call from Aiden. Aiden is one of my closest guy friends, and he and Chris are best friends.

"Hey, Aiden! How are you?" I asked.

"Good, but I can't say the same for Chris," he answered.

"This is why you called me Aiden… really, wow!"

"Asia, it's not like that, alright," "I just want to let you know that I am not taking sides between you and Chris. I just really want to fix things between you guys. Plus, I really don't want our group to be affected because of you two's break up,"

Aiden is always trying to be the peacemaker in our group; it's really sweet that he cares, but sometimes he shouldn't get involved in things like this.

"Thank you, Aiden, Goodnight!" I said in a sing-song type of voice.

"Hold up! Asia, when are you leaving?"

"I'm leaving in one more day. It's that all? Great goodbye," I answered for him.

"You make him Crazy, Asia, like you're his drug or something," Aiden lightly chuckled.

Whoa! No way! I can't believe this.

"Aiden wha—"

"Goodnight, Asia," Aiden said and hung up on me.

Wow, I never knew Chris cared for me like that, this is so unbelievable, but I am not going back to him. My mind is made up, and that's final. Aiden really got my head spinning with thoughts about Chris. Ugh! Why did he have to tell me that?

"Dwayne, you need to stop this; you're behaving like a grown-ass toddler. She is our daughter, and don't ignore her because of this one incident," I heard my mom tell my dad.

"I can't face her, Janiya. That was my baby girl in that room, ready to become an adult," My dad said.

My heart sank, and it felt like I was going through a hole.

"Honey, I understand how you fee—"

"No, you don't, Jay. Instead of punishing her bad behavior, you reward her," my dad said.

"I can't punish her for wanting to have sex, Dwayne; I can only tell how to protect herself," she said. "She also told me that they didn't do anything," she said.

"I'll try to talk to her"

"You better, because ignoring her is not going to solve anything but get you in trouble with me," My mom barks.

"I'll talk to her before or after family dinner," My dad told her.

Crap, I totally forgot about the family dinner tomorrow. I can't wait to see my older brother Marcus and his girlfriend Champagne. I'm really stoked about going to Africa. This trip will give my parents and me some bonding time. I woke up this morning with the house smelling like a mouth-watering aroma. The aroma smells so good I can taste it in my mouth. I went downstairs to help my mother prepare our food.

"Good morning, momma," I said.

"Good morning? It's the afternoon," My mom said. "You overslept," she said.

"It's there anything I can help you with?" I asked.

"You can set up the table at the lake house"

The lake house is so far I wish I never opened my big mouth. I had to walk a long-ass walk from my house and to the lake house. When I arrived at the lake house, I saw my dad setting up the table.

"Go get ready; I got this," My dad said.

"Okay, thank you," I said.

He didn't say anything back. He couldn't even look at me in my eyes. I had to walk all the long-ass walk back to my house. I put my hair in a bun. I picked out a nice outfit; it's a white dress with a jean jacket. I also wore silver hoop earrings; I did my makeup. I walked to my lake house looking and feeling cute.

At the lake house, everything looks so exquisite, and the food looks mouthwatering. I checked the large dining table. There is a big turkey like its thanksgiving. I swear only our family has thanksgiving in July.

"Asia, don't drool. Come help me and your father put the rest of the food on the table," My momma said.

I'm not allowed to eat the food until my other family members show up, which sucks ass because I am hungry as hell. The first guest who arrived is my older sister Maysie, and she is wearing white too.

"Hey Maysie, you look really gorgeous," I told her.

"Asia, trust me, it's all you," She complimented me.

"Thank you, thank you," I flaunted.

About fifty minutes later, the whole family arrived, and they are all wearing white. It's an unspoken dress code that no one asked for.

"Was there a dress code or something?" My grandma Betty questioned.

"No, mom, there is no dress code," My dad said.

"Oh good, I thought Janiya didn't tell me to make me look like a fool, thank goodness that didn't happen because I wore white," My grandma Betty said.

"How dare you talk about my daughter like that?" Nana Jahzara asked.

"You know damn well; my daughter wouldn't do such a thing," Nana Jahzara spoke.

Drama is beginning, and every time it turns into something bigger than it needs to be. The doorbell rang, and I excused myself from the table. I refuse to get dragged into any family drama. I'm so grateful for whoever rang the doorbell, but I hate the fact that I had to walk from the lake house to the main house.

"Oh, it's you," I said.

"Is that how you say hi?" Aiden asked.

"Well, don't stand there. Come inside," I told him.

"Don't get mad, but I invited Chris," Aiden said as Chris walked towards us.

"You have a lot of balls showing up here after what happened the other day," I told Chris.

"Asia, I wanted to see you before you left, and I didn't want you to leave for two weeks knowing that you're angry at me," Chris said.

"Come in… both of you," I said.

Chris and Aiden both had grins on their faces. We went upstairs and into my room.

"What do you guys want to do?" I asked them.

"Asia, are you okay that I'm here? If it isn't, I'll leave," Chris spoke.

"I let you in, didn't I?"

"Let's play **UNO** while listening to old school," Aiden said.

"Prepare to lose," Chris jokes.

Aiden played the song Unwritten by Natasha Bedingfield. As soon as the song started playing, Chris started blushing. I smiled at Chris; this is the song we had our first kiss in the 7th grade.

"Aww, look at you both blushing at this song that's so cute," Aiden jest.

Aiden is so irritating he knows the history Chris and I have with this song.

"Aiden, shut up."

16

I threw a pillow at him, and we all started laughing. We played several rounds of **UNO**, and Chris lost each round. It was sad and cute at the same time because he always had hope that he'd win the next round.

"Since I won most of the rounds, I get to choose what we do next, and I want to watch the *sisterhood of traveling pants,*" I said.

"No, not that movie," Chris whined.

"Why? Because you're scared that you're going to cry in front of Aiden".

Aiden started laughing so hard.

"Seriously, dude, you actually cry while watching the sisterhood of the traveling pants" Aiden said.

"No," Chris lied.

"Chris, no need to lie, you always cry when Tibby's mom gets the phone call that Bailey dies.

"Okay fine, I cry, so what's a very melancholy moment in the movie? Aiden was dying with laughter, and Chris was just really embarrassed. We watched the movie while all three of us lay on my bed. I cried when Tibby went to Bailey at the hospital. Chris cuddled me and wrapped His arms around me. A few hours later, I woke up and found myself around Chris's arms around my waist and Aiden's feet close to my face. The position that I woke to was so weird, but yet I felt comfortable. Even though Aiden's feet were close to my face, I felt comfortable because I was in his arms. I turned my Body facing Chris instead of Aiden's feet. I studied Chris's face while he was sleeping. He is so beautiful. This is the point of my life, wondering if I did the right thing by breaking up with him. I mean, what relationship doesn't go through ups and downs. *Did I give up on us too soon? Was it wrong that I was happy that he came with Aiden?*

I don't know what I was thinking, but I found my lips on his. Chris woke up smiling and kissed me back. The kiss was fiery and hot. We made out until we fell off my bed and onto the floor. We chuckled quietly, to not wake up Aiden. I know I was the one who dumped him, but I want to rip off his clothes. I kissed him again and more gently.

"Aww, look at the two love birds," Aiden said from on top of my bed. "I hope you guys weren't planning to have sex while I'm in here; actually, never mind, I want to watch," Aiden said.

"Ewe, no, Aiden, we weren't going to," I said.

"Asia, are you awake?" my dad said, knocking at the door.

"Hide," I whispered to both Aiden and Chris.

"Where?" questioned Aiden.

"Under the bed in my closet, I don't care as long as he doesn't see you. Chris went under my Bed, and Aiden went into my closet.

"May I come in?" my dad asked.

"Yah, sure, dad."

"Can you turn down the music, please?"

"Sure," I answered while turning down the music.

"Malaysia, I know I've been kind of an asshole," my dad spoke.

"Kind of?"

"Alright, fine, I've behaved like a total asshole or, like your mom said, a grown-ass toddler," said my dad. "Asia, you're my baby girl, and it's hard for me to see that you're growing up, and I know that part of growing up is to want to have sex even though I know this is hard for me to accept because Malaysia you sister Maysie got pregnant at an early age of fifteen but then she had a miscarriage. Because of that she was really depressed, blamed it on herself, and she was also suicidal. I'm trying to create that I don't want the same thing to happen to you. As a father who loves his children deeply, Asia is a hard thing to watch them suffer and not knowing How to make it stop."

Woah, I would've never imagined that my dad thinks about stuff like this. That's crazy.

"Dad, to be completely honest, I think I wouldn't be able to call myself a virgin if mom didn't walk in on us, and I know that this conversation is hard and awkward for you as it is for me, but I feel like I should be honest because you have the right for me not to lie to. I also want to let you know that I know what Maysie went through, but dad, I want to let you know that I'm not her."

"Malaysia, I understand that you're not here but the baby of this family, so it is hard and especially me seeing you in that position with that Mitchel kid."

I gave him a hug and told him that I was growing and experiencing the world.

"Get some sleep; we have an early flight in the morning," my dad said and gently closed the door.

Aiden and Chris came from where they were hiding. The room was completely quiet until Aiden got a phone call from his mom telling him he needs to come home.

"This was fun, but I got to blast, Chris. Are you coming"?

"Nah, I'll just stay with her for a little bit," Chris said.

"Don't get caught sneaking out," I told Aiden.

"I never get caught," Aiden said and walked out.

"Are you sure you don't want to go home and be with Addison Miller?" I said in a valley girl voice.

"Come on, Malaysia, now you're being petty,"

I didn't say anything after that.

"I'm here with you, Malaysia Strawberry Johnson, and not with Addy," he says and kisses me. "Asia, what are we...like a relationship like...I mean you dumped less than 24 hours ago, but then you kissed me which I'm not complaining about," Chris said.

"Why did you have to say my middle name Straw-berry...I told you my parents were under the influence of crack cocaine when naming me Strawberry,"

"No, they were in the influence of very expensive Strawberry champagne while making you, so they decided to name you after the flavor of champagne they drank," "I should have never told you that," I said.

"I like the name Strawberry. I think it is cute".

"No, when you think Strawberry, you think Strawberry shortcake. I don't want to be known as a Strawberry shortcake"

"Well then, you're lucky your name is not Strawberry Malaysia Johnson...stop changing the subject," He said.

Crap, I was trying to avoid this confusion because he's right and to be totally honest, I don't know where Chris and my relationship stand. Sometimes I can't stand myself; I can't believe I'm doing this to him.

"Look, Chris, I...I...I don't know, okay! I don't know! I broke up with you yesterday because all my emotions were—"

He didn't really have anything to say after that he was speechless.

"Chris, how about you give me the two weeks that I'm away to think about our relationship and where we stand, then when I come back, my mind will be made up,"

Chris gave me a peck on the lips and told me goodnight.

"Let me walk you out; it's almost twelve o'clock," I said. We walked outside until Chris stopped in front of my neighbor's house.

"Asia, you should go back inside," Chris said.

"Chris, are you mad at me?"

"No, not at you...at myself for letting our relationship become so confusing to you that you don't know what you want," he spoke.

"Don't knock yourself down, Chris"

"Malaysia, I want to be and stay in a relationship with you that you're positive about, not in a relationship where you have to think about staying in," Chris said.

I didn't know what to say. It's my fault, and I feel bad.

"Asia, don't feel so bad...uhm...how about when you come back, we have an 80's movie Marathon.... Even if you don't want to be in a relationship with me," Chris said.

"It's a date,"

He kissed my cheek and left. I went to my room to have a good night's sleep, but I saw Koko bear sleeping on my bed. She's so cute. I totally am going to miss her, but Maysie promised to take good care of her. She will pick her up after she drops us off at the airport. In the morning, everything was hectic; mom was double no triple-checking to make sure everyone had everything we needed.

"Honey, calm down; we have everything we need for the trip," my dad told my mom.

"Where the hell is Maysie?" My mom questioned.

"I swear if we miss our flight because of her—"

"For goodness sake, Sweetie, she's on her way, remember we have traffic." My dad said, the doorbell rang, and it was Maysie.

"Maysie, thank god you're here. Mom was literally freaking out". I told Maysie.

"She's just nervous because she's going on the plan for about 24 hours," Maysie said. I completely forgot about my mom's fear of heights.

"Mom do you have your pills?" asked Maysie.

"Why did you say it like that?" My mom questioned

"Say it like what?"

"Mom, do you have your pills" my mom mimicked Maysie.

"Honey, deep breaths, it's okay she was just worried," my dad said in a calming voice.

The whole car ride, mom was praying so we don't get in a plane crash.

"Next time, Asia, make sure you remind me not to give mom a car ride to the airport," Maysie said as she hugged me goodbye.

"One last thing, please take care of Koko bear. She's really shy, and she doesn't like being bothered. I left you her summer schedule. Make sure you follow it, or else she will get very fussy and will make your life a living hell." I explained to her.

"You make Koko sound like a spoiled brat," Maysie said.

"She's not spoiled. She just likes things in certain ways, or else she'll get mad," I told her.

"I'll try to stay on schedule anyway. You guys have fun; don't do anything too crazy and please be careful," Maysie said to us.

When we arrived, I was so tired I didn't get a chance to enjoy our beautiful plaza hotel. As soon as I reached my hotel room, I was knocked out.

"Honey, wake up," my mom said.

``Momma, it's too early for this," I grumble.

"It's noon. We are behind our schedule, so get up and get ready," she said and left.

I did exactly what she said I got ready. We originally planned on eating breakfast in the hotel, but we decided to eat at a restaurant close by. The restaurant we decided to stop by was very fancy plus it was really close to the hotel. My parents and I had a wonderful conversation in French. My dad said we are in a country with people who speak French; why not speak the language if we all know it. My family and I speak several different languages because of my parents' love for traveling. They wanted us to be able to communicate with different people with different languages and cultures. I think the family bonding thing is going great for the three of us.

After our delicious breakfast, we decided to go to Cathédrale, which was close by. The Cathédrale is this beautiful Catholic Church. I was really fascinated by this beauty. We met this old guy. He was really sweet, and he was telling us about it. He said he could tell that we're foreigners and gave us advice on where to go and told us the best public transportation to use is a taxi. We've been using a taxi all along, so I was glad that we were doing something right. We decided to go to the Pierre Savorgnan de Brazza Memorial. The building taught us a lot about a man named Brazza and the history of Brazzaville. We got hungry again, so we decided to stop by a restaurant around us. The restaurant is very well known in Brazzaville. It had great food that we stuffed our faces with. I wanted to go to the poto-poto market.

"Malaysia, don't wander off like you usually do," My mom said.

I don't mean to wander off. I just get fascinated with things, and my attention is drawn to them, so I usually get lost or don't know where my parents are at the time.

Around the time we reached the market, it was late but not that late as if everyone went home. We saw a lot of beautiful jewelry, and I was really awestruck with one. I asked the woman in French how much it cost. It cost about 5,350.78 CFA, which is 10 dollars. It was pretty cheap but lovely.

When I was done buying, I looked up to look for my parents, but they were gone, and I couldn't find them. This is exactly what my parents were talking about. No wonder they say that they can't take me places because I'll be behaving like a five-year-old. I tried to yell for their names, but I couldn't find them.

The place was packed but not as packed as it would usually be because it was the evening.

"Mom, Dad, where are you?" I called out like an idiot.

I tried asking people if they've seen them. I tried my best to describe how they looked in French, but no one saw them. What have I gotten myself into? I can't believe I got lost in another country by not following my parents' simple instructions. I'm 16 going on 17, but I behave like I'm five. Damn it, I'm lost, and it's getting really dark.

"Momma! Dad! Momma! Dad!" I called.

CHRISTOPHER

"Daddy, are you still moping over that bitch? When you could have me here right now," Addy said.

"Addison, I don't have time for your bullshit," I told her.

"That's not what you said last time, you," she said and smacked her itty-bitty behind.

"Please leave and close the door on your way out."

"Baby, don't worry, you'll come around, and when you do, you'll member how sweet my kitty is," Addy said and left.

Man, you hit one time, and now she thinks she's all bad and whatnot.

"Christopher Ryan Mitchell, what did we tell you about being nice to Addison"? My mom asked, Barging into my room. Did she really snitch on me to my parents?

"You said to be nice and do what she tells you to"

"That's right; we really need this business deal, and the only way to get it is for her to be a guest in our home while her parents are away," my father said.

"But she's really annoying and getting on my nerves"

"But you guys were really close. What happened?" my mom asked.

"People change," I answered.

"She told us that your girlfriend dumped you, and you're behaving really impertinent toward her," my mom said.

"Malaysia and I didn't break up; it's complicated," I said.

"We don't care, just work it out with her and do whatever she tells you to," said my father.

I knew my parents didn't care about my personal life. All they care about is money. On their way out, I heard my mother tell my dad that she never really liked Malaysia. But I honestly have no idea why Malaysia is really the sweetest person I met. I also know that she's behaving this way because I hurt her a lot. That's why I'm being patient and waiting for her to make her decision. I have to leave my house, so I went for a jog to get away from the craziness that's happening in my house. After the jog, I took a long ass shower.

"Addy, what are you doing in my room"? I asked.

"I'm here for you," She said and took off the silk robe she had on. "Come on, baby. I know you want this," "Take that towel off," she said.

I heard a knock on my door.

"Hey man, your mom let me innnnnnnnn '' Aiden said, unsettle. "Are you kidding me? She is gone in less than a week, and you're already tapping Addy," Aiden said.

"It's not what it looks like," I said.

"Addy's naked, and you're in your towel, claiming it is not what it looks like," spoke Aiden.

After Aiden said that, Addy put her robes back on.

"I get that you and Asia aren't best friends anymore, but she'll never do anything like this to you," Aiden said.

Addy's face changed color, and she left the room.

"As for you, man, I'm really disappointed in man; a few days ago I was telling Asia how you guys are such a great couple, and you guys should stay together…but now, man, I don't even know anymore you're digging yourself deep especially with someone she used to mess with,"

26

"Man, I just came out of the shower, and I saw her in my room with her clothes off; trust me, nothing happened, man," I explain.

"Be completely honest; if I never came, would you have smashed?" He questioned.

"I don't know, maybe...I mean...no...yes...she came onto me, okay, and I'm a horny teenager,"

"That's your lame ass excuse...but alright, man, I'm leaving," He said.

"Aiden, please don't mention this to Malaysia".

"Alright, man but Asia, she's crazy about you, dude. I swear you're like her drug or something," he said and left.

I put on some clothes, but I couldn't help but think about what Aiden said. Is Asia really that crazy about me?

"Chris, your parents just left, and they wanted me to tell you," Addy said.

"What do you mean, my parents just left?"

"Your parents got a call from my parents, and they said they had to leave. It was an emergency,"

"My parents just left us like this?" I asked.

"No, they asked me if we wanted to go...but I said no," Addy explained

"Did they at least tell you where they are going, and how long?"

"They went to Japan, but I don't know for how long," she explained and left.

I went to sleep, but I kept on having nightmares of Malaysia like she was in some kind of danger. It's so crazy because it felt so real; maybe it is my guilty conscience. I kept on hearing ringing. I finally realize that it's my phone ringing.

"Hello, is this Chris?" Said a similar voice on the other line.

"Yeah, who is this"? I asked.

"This is Maysie, Malaysia's older sister"

"Hi Maysie, how have you been?"

"Good, is Malaysia at your house?" she questioned.

"What…what do you mean?"

"Is Asia my little sister at your house?" she questioned rudely.

"She is in Brazzaville, not in my house"

"I'm sorry for the way I acted."

"It's all good, no stress"

"No, it's not. It's Asia she is missing," She said.

What the sentence she said took me a minute to fully get what she said.

"Asia, my girlfriend, Asia, is missing?" I questioned.

"Yah, I thought maybe she got bored and took a flight here," She said.

"Come on, Maysie Malaysia is not that irresponsible, and I know she would've considered your parents' feelings," I told her.

"You're right, Chris. I'm scared, and I'm worried about her. She's my baby sister," She told me.

"Are you going to Brazzaville?"

"Yah, my flight leaves at night," She said

"Maysie, I have to go but can you send me the Hotel address to the hotel your parents are staying at?"

She said okay and hung up.

I went into my closet to pack as many clothes that fit in my suitcase and some deodorant, toothpaste, toothbrush.

"I'm coming," Addy said.

"Addy, this is no time for your bullshit. You don't even like Malaysia, and she could be in danger,"

"I'm not messing with you. I know Asia and I are not on the best of terms right now, but we have a history where we were once best friends. She was like a sister to me once, and I know you don't trust my intentions, but she could be endangered. I'm putting everything that happened behind us and I'm willing to help look for her, plus you could use my parent's private plane," She explained.

I told her alright, and we got ready. When we arrived, we took the taxi to the address that Maysie sent to me. We got separate rooms. I felt like it wasn't right for us to share a room. In the morning, after we ate breakfast, we went to the check-in to ask what room, but they said they couldn't give us that information.

"Christopher, Addison, what are you kids doing here?" asked Mrs. Johnson.

"We came to help search for Malaysia," Addy answered.

"How did you guys find out about Asia being missing"? Mr. Johnson asked.

"Maysie called me and asked if she flew back to the United States to see me, but she didn't," I explained.

"Why are you here, Addison?" Mrs. Johnson asked.

"I overheard him talking to Maysie on the phone," she answered.

Mrs. Johnson had a question on her face.

"She's staying at my place while her parents are away on a business trip," I told them.

"Do your parents even know that you're here?" Mr. Johnson asked.

"Our parents are aware that we are here, and they are totally okay with it," Addy lied.

I feel uncomfortable lying to Asia's parents like that.

"Where's Maysie?" I asked to change the subject.

"She's at the airport, and we were going to the airport to get her. You children should come," Mrs. Johnson said.

We agree to go with them.

"Aiden's flight should have arrived by now," Addy whispered.

"Aiden! What is he doing here?

"Did I forget to mention that I told him that Malaysia is missing in another country, so he bought the first plane ticket to here," Addy said.

"How come you never brought this up to me?" I ask.

"I just did," she said.

"When we arrived at the airport, we saw Maysie and Marcus,

but Marcus kept on staring at Addy and me. I think he probably knew I cheated on Asia with Addy.

"So, you told complete strangers that Malaysia is missing, but you couldn't even tell your son her brother that she was missing," Marcus said to his parents.

Oh crap, his parents didn't tell him. That is crazy.

"Son, don't get all worked up; we just weren't trying to worry; that's all," Mr. Johnson said.

"Bullshit! That's complete bullshit!" Marcus yelled.

"I'm going to look for Aiden. His flight should have landed," Addy whispered in my ear.

I would have gone with her, but the Johnsons would've realized we both were gone, so I decided to stay.

"Marcus, we didn't want to worry you, honestly. Basketball season is coming up, so we didn't want to distract you; that's all," Mrs. Johnson said.

"You got to be kidding; my sister's safety is way more important than basketball; what do you guys take me for?!" Marcus yelled.

"Hey, don't you dare use that tone at us. We get it; you're pissed. But the important thing is you're here, and you're going to help search for your sister," Mr. Johnson said.

"Thanks to Maysie, I could be here to help look for Asia," Marcus said.

It was ironically funny that all said they needed a shower before looking for her. After they finished, we went down to the police station, which already had a search team looking for her. Marcus, Maysie, Addy, Aiden and I and some policemen were looking for her. Mrs. Johnson and Mr. Johnson, and a few policemen went searching for Asia. I didn't speak any French so I couldn't understand what the policemen were saying. They suspected that Malaysia might have gotten missing in the forest.

"I hate the rainforest. I'm like an all you can eat buffet for bugs," Addy complained.

"Girl, you out her worrying about bugs, and I'm out here worrying about leopards and shit trying to make me their dinner," Maysie complained.

The rainforest is magnificent, and I felt safe with policemen with guns, and they knew their way around the country. I tried talking to Marcus, but I could tell he didn't really mess with me.

"Isn't this so beautiful, Marcus?" I asked.

"Leave me alone and look for my sister," he responded.

I could tell that Addy was attracted to Asia's brother. When Marcus would look her way, she would just blush, and when Marcus would look away, she would just gaze at him. I could tell Maysie didn't like Addison. When she would try to talk to her, she would just have an irritated look on her face.

"It's late; we have to continue our search for the girl tomorrow," one of the policeman said.

"No, we have to continue. We can't just go back," Maysie argued.

"You guys can't do this. We just can't stop," Marcus said.

"Late, we will look for the girl tomorrow," he said.

"I guess I'm staying here and continuing looking for my sister," Maysie.

"I'm with her," Marcus said.

"Me too," Aiden, Addy, and I said as one.

"You kids have to go with the policemen so you guys can get to the hotel safely."

"No offense, Maysie, but I'm not going back to the hotel. I didn't travel all the way here to look for Malaysia and turn back away," I said.

"Sorry, Maysie, I'm with Chris on this one," Aiden said.

"Alright, fine, but you guys need to realize that the possible danger that you're putting yourself in and that the policemen are obviously going with their truck, so we are going to be walking the rest of the way. We only have a map and no weapons to protect us," Maysie said.

"We have protection," Marcus said and pulled out a gun.

"Marcus, what in the world are you doing with a gun?" Maysie questioned.

"Asia could've been kidnapped. You expect me not to walk around with protection just in case," he answered.

Maysie explained to the policemen what we decided on in French. Only one policeman decided to stay. He looked young like he just joined the force.

"My name is Raymond, but you can call me Ray," Ray said in a British accent.

"Why did you decide to stay with us?" Questioned Maysie.

"Because I want to help look for your sister," Ray answered with a sarcastic tone.

"Bro, you didn't need to answer her question like that. She was just curious," Marcus told him.

"I was just answering the question, so stop trying to start shit. Your behavior is so childish," Ray said.

"Don't say nothing back, Marcus, just let him be," Maysie said.

I tried talking to Aiden, but he kept on ignoring me. When I would try to make conversation, he would just talk to Maysie.

"*I'm* drain*ed*. Can we please rest here? We have been walking for hours," Addy whined.

"Yah, we should rest. We have a long way ahead before we reach the village," Ray said.

We made a fire, and we ate and drank water. While everyone fell asleep, I couldn't, so I stayed up. I just hope Malaysia is okay. I hope she is safe. I just want to hold her in my arms and tell her I love her.

"You're still awake?" asked Addy.

"Addy, you should go back to sleep,"

"Come on, let me keep you company," She took my silence as yes.

"You must be thinking about *Asia*," She said.

"Addy, what are you doing here"? I asked.

"I'm sitting here with you by the fire. *That's what I'm* doing here," She answered.

"No, I mean, why are you here in Congo looking for *Asia...* Don't you hate her?"

"I don't hate *Asia. I* could never hate *her*," she told me.

"I don't get you, *Addison*," I said.

"You won't understand, Chris, trust me on that," she said.

"Addy, you can tell me anything you know that we were once friends," I told her.

"I LIKE *Malaysia*," she said.

"You just told me that," I said.

"No, Chris, I have feelings for her," Addison said.

"What, this makes zero sense? You have feelings for me. You had sex with me," I said baffled.

"I'm bisexual," she said with relief.

I'm glad she came out to me.

"When I moved from New York to California, I had a hard time making friends, and Malaysia became my friend, not only a friend, my best friend. Asia was my first female crush. I didn't know what to do; I couldn't believe the feelings I have for her. I remember I used to like her so much I used to copy whatever she did, and when she said she liked something, I would like it too. I remember I used to be so jealous of Keisha because she and Asia had a bond. I remember when Malaysia first started liking you. I used to dislike you so much I was angry at you, and at Malaysia, I was angry at you because you weren't all that, and I was angry at Malaysia because why couldn't she have feelings for me like she had feelings for you. I Sort of got over her liking you, so I told Asia and Keisha I liked you too one day. Oh my god, you should have seen Asia. She was angry and sad. She said I broke the girl code, and she said I wouldn't have liked you if she never had a crush on you. She was right; I never liked you at all. I honestly couldn't believe why she liked you. Keisha kept on telling Asia that I just wanted to be her, which wasn't true because I just wanted to be with her. I remember our seventh-grade dance like it was yesterday. I got so jealous when I saw you guys dancing together, and then when you guys kissed, I was heartbroken; Chris, I was heartbroken. I went home crying, yelling, and breaking stuff. I hated you at that time. I have never hated anyone before, but Chris, I hated you. Asia and Keisha, and I didn't really talk to each other much after that dance. I couldn't look her in the eyes. My heart was so torn. Then we went to high school. I still didn't like you. In fact, I despise you. We were in Mrs. Stuart's class when you started talking to me, and then we became friends, and that's when I developed feelings for you, but you were dating Asia. I didn't want to believe I developed feelings for her boyfriend. I knew that Asia was jealous of our friendship, and she had every right. I mean, you did end up cheating on her with me. But anyway, I was so happy that she had a taste of how I felt for years. That's why I'm petty all the time; my big-time crush for Malaysia gets my adrenaline pumping," Explained Addison.

"Wow, Addison, I don't know what to say," I said, stunned. The way Addison speaks of Malaysia is as if she is in love with her, and that's crazy.

"Did you come out to your parents, or I'm the first person you told?" I asked.

"I came out to my parents. I told them I was bisexual, but they told me that I was confused, and I was influenced by what I see on the internet". I could hear the pain in her voice when she spoke.

"I don't think you're confused. I believe you know that you're bi and not influenced by what you see on the internet," "Addison, can I ask you a question?" I ask.

"You just did, but I suppose you can ask me another one," she told me.

"When you came into my room in your robe the other day, what were you thinking"?

"I knew that I caused you and Asia to break, so I was trying to do that again, and I wanted to get laid," she admitted.

"Damn, that's messed up,"

"I know, but Chris, you have no idea how it feels to love someone, but they're in love with someone else," she explained.

"Addison, you love Malaysia!" I exclaimed.

"What nooo…. yes, I do, but I also have feelings for someone else " she said. "I know I know I'm a hot mess," "Listen, Chris, I trust you, so please don't tell anyone what I told you,".

"Don't worry, I won't,"

"Chris, I'm going to bed. You should too," she said.

"I will, but first, I'm going to get more wood for the fire so the mosquito can be attracted to the heat," I told her.

I'm terrified I'm out of my mind walking in the woods alone with zero protection. But if the bugs attract the heat or light, plus we also have on bug spray, we'll be protected from getting bitten.

"Oh shit! Oh shit! "I said out loud with excitement to myself.

I found tracks; I found tire tracks. I think this would be really helpful to find Malaysia. I was so excited I did a little happy dance. This could be a lead on where Malaysia is heading towards. I tripped on a tree stub and heard my bone crack. I had never heard a human bone crack before, and my bone cracked. The pain I'm feeling is unbelievable. I had never felt something like this

"Help! Help! Somebody help me please!" I shout.

But no one heard me. I'm in so much pain I felt like I was going to pass out, scraped myself, and I was hurting all over. I could barely walk with the stick. I was just glad it was thick enough to hold my weight.

"Maysie! Marcus! Aiden! Addison! Ray! Someone, please help me!" I yelled so loud I could feel my lungs hurt. "Someone, please help. I don't want to die!" I bellowed.

I tried looking for the fire or the place where we set up, but I couldn't. I didn't know where to go. I'm going to die in these woods, and I didn't even get a chance to find Malaysia. I didn't get a chance to tell her I love her more than anyone in the world. I now know what I had, but I ruined it. I took advantage without realizing I was taking advantage, but now it's gone. I had a great life, a wonderful girlfriend, a wealthy family, and how could I have gone wrong. I heard hissing noises, please don't be a snake, and please don't be a snake. It's a snake; I'm going to be turned into snake food.

"Somebody, please save me. I'm going to die!" I shout.

"He's down there," I heard someone say.

Thank goodness I'm going to be saved. I saw two people coming, and it was Marcus and Aiden.

"How did you end up here?" asked Marcus.

"I'll tell you after I become snake food!" I yelled.

"Oh right," Marcus said and shot the snake.

"What the heck, man? Isn't that illegal?!" I said.

"Yah, no sweat, but man, what happened to your leg?" Marcus asked.

"I don't even know one minute I was getting more wood for the fire, and the next minute I was tripping, and I heard my bone cracked," I explained.

"That looks pretty bad. We need to take you to the doctor, man," Aiden said.

"Yah, your leg looks bad. It's purple and swollen," Marcus said.

"It looks nasty, but the pain I'm feeling it's something else," I told them.

They carried me back to where we were camping.

"Christopher!" Maysie yelled.

"Omg! Chris, are you okay?" Addy yelled.

"I'm alive, but okay, that's something I'm not feeling," I told her.

"I'm glad you're alive, but we need to take you to the hospital, and we can't turn back," Maysie said.

I didn't say anything. Why did I have to be the person that always creates problems for everyone?

"Maybe we should split up half of us and continue the search for Asia and the rest go with Chris to the hospital," Maysie suggested.

"That's a horrible idea," Ray said.

"How about you come up with a better idea?" Maysie told him.

"Your idea is bad because we are closer to the town than to the city, and we are going to carry him. We have no vehicle to take us there, plus we are going to have to carry him, which will slow us down. I believe the smartest idea is to go to the village even though it's a far walk, but it's closer than the city," Ray suggested.

"I agree with the sexy British guy," Addy said.

"I'm sorry, Maysie, me too," said Aiden.

"I'm going with Ray on this one," I told her.

"What about you, Marcus? What do you think about this?" Maysie asked her older brother.

"I agree with him because he knows the way around here, and we don't," Marcus said.

"Alright, Ray, I guess we follow your lead," Maysie said.

"I have painkillers in my *book bag*," Ray said.

"Chris, here, put this in your mouth because you're going to need i**t.**"

MALAYSIA

I slowly opened my eyes, finally opened as the pain in my head dulled and settled into a dull ringing in my ears. Terror building, I glanced ruefully at the chains bonds that held me back that turned out to be chains shackled to my wrists, defying any hope of escape. My legs felt like jelly as I stood. As I reached out for support, I felt the coldness of the wrought iron bars that made up the walls of the cage in which I stood. It was one of several; there were others like me -- confused captives. I twisted my wrists in a desperate effort to ease them out, but it was no use. Clenching my teeth together, I tried again, but the results were the same. "So, you're the one who tried to escape," came a voice from behind me. I turned and examined the man, conscious of the tightening in my jaw. "Quite a beauty, you are." A foreigner, just like me." He smirked at me before continuing, "It's my first time doing business here. I'm glad that I had an opportunity to enjoy such a sight.

Silence hung in the air for a moment before he snapped his fingers, prompting two men to emerge and remove my binds. I didn't fight them. I learned my lesson from the last time I tried. The dark stranger snapped his fingers once more, and one of the men hauled me up and carried me out of the cage. I wanted to hiss and squeal but felt I was far too weak. As the man carried me through a gated doorway and down a dark alley, my eyes began to flicker, exhaustion setting in. *It's too dangerous to fall asleep.* I reminded myself. *Where am I? Are they going to punish me again? Wasn't the last beating punishment enough?* After a while, the men stopped. I was flung onto the floor like a rag doll. "Gentle," the mysterious man said. "Sorry, boss."

I looked around surreptitiously. This place was nicer than the filthy cages I'd woken in. It even smelled cleaner, cleaner, at least. "Call Esmeralda," the dark stranger boomed. A pregnant girl with long and luscious dark locks appeared with food. I couldn't help but notice how tired she looked. She set a plate of food beside me, which I attacked like a ravenous hyena. The crowd of people stared at me while I devoured my food, but I didn't care; I hadn't eaten in days and had never been so hungry. After I'd finished, Esmeralda was told to clean me up. Taking me by the hand, she walked me to the bathroom. Esmeralda didn't speak and wouldn't look me directly in the eyes. After I was done, she walked me back to where we first met. Most of the men had left, with only the mysterious man remaining.

"You look more beautiful than ever, Malaysia." My jaw clenched as he spoke my name. Esmeralda skulked off, leaving just the two of us. "Malaysia, Malaysia!" he repeated. *Who is he? Have I met this man before? Why is he saying my name as if we've known one another for a lifetime?* I shivered at the feel of his hands caressing my back. He leaned in and whispered in my ear, his jagged stubble pricking my cheek. I turned and looked into his eyes. I saw hunger. Heated desire. Lust. He looked at me like he was ready to devour me. I knew what was about to happen, though I refused to let him have his way. Punched him as hard as I could in his face, and ran. "You're a feisty one," he chuckled from behind me. "Get her!" I kept on running but was stopped by a wall of huge men. You can't run from me, Malaysia," he called. "Leave me alone!" I yelled, fighting the buildup of "Leave me alone!" I yelled, fighting the buildup of hot tears. "I own you, sweetheart. You can't tell me what to do!" "Please, let me go," I pleaded. He snorted derisively before turning to look at his men. "Leave us," he told them. "And you," he said, looking back at me, "If you try that again, things won't end well for you."

A few hours later

"Take her away. I'm finished with her." Without a word, a man picked me up and carried me away. There was no cage this time; he dropped into a place full of people. As I glanced around the room, I saw a little girl huddled in a corner, sitting cradling her legs. She looked to be around 5 or 6 years old, and the sight of her frightened little form was enough to cause tears to cascade down my cheeks. *How can they be so cruel? She is just a little girl!* Looking over at her, I was suddenly overcome by a burning need to protect this petrified little girl. I approached her, cautiously, "Hi, do you speak English?" I asked. The little girl responded with a tentative nod. "My name is Malaysia," I said. What's your name?" After a slight pause, she spoke in a mousey voice: "My name is Andrea." She flinched as she spoke as if startled by her own voice and patently scared of her own shadow

"Can I call you Drea," I asked. "Only my friends call me that," she replied. "Can I be your friend?" I questioned. She nods again. "How old are you, Drea?" "I am five" "How old are you?" She asked, "I am 16," I told her. A few minutes later, a man came and snatched Andrea. "Leave me alone!" She squealed. "Help me!" "Stop, let her go!" I went up to the man, and I started attacking the man; I didn't care if he is way bigger than me. I looked around, and no one else moved to help this helpless child. "Come on, people, let's help her," I cried. Some of them looked away, and some just kept on starting. "Please let me go," she cried. "Somebody help me" I continue to hit the man, but he wouldn't Budge, but I can tell that he is getting annoyed with me. I notice that when the girl keeps on yelling, she never yelled for her parents, which I find peculiar. The man dropped Drea and grabbed me by my hair. He yanked my hair as he pulled me on the cold concrete floor. "Leave her alone!" says the frail little girl. "Drea, it's fine, go sit down, please," I pleaded with her. Tears welled from deep inside and coursed down her cheeks. The man continued to drag me by my hair and into a dark alley as I cried out in excruciating pain.

I couldn't move and couldn't talk. All I was doing was crying.

"Look who I brought" the man who held my hair showed me off.

"This little brat got in my way; she is lucky that I didn't hurt her."

The man said while chaining me up to the wall. The chains on my neck feel uncomfortable.

"Don't think about it, or else you will become like Derrick or worse."

"You know she is his new favorite toy."

"I don't know what he sees in her"

"I do."

"She looks delicious," said one of the men.

The others chuckled.

"You know we're not allowed to touch her," he said.

"Good, I'm glad you remember," The boss said.

"What did you do this time?" The boss said as he approached me.

"She got in my way when I was trying to take the little girl,"

The man answered the question. "Is that so?" "Yes, sir" "Okay, I will deal with her later, but first, let's take about the Europe business trip," He said. I sat there listening to them discuss us going to Europe, then Asia, and then the Americas. They talked about which girls they were going to sell. They also talked about how we were going to leave for Italy in a few days.

There's no way in hell I'm going to Italy with them. I need to escape, and I'm taking Andrea with me. How I'm going to escape? There are a lot of them, and it's only Andrea and me. After they were finished, the boss took the chains off me. "Follow me," The boss told me. I did l as I was told. We entered; the mysterious man is in a private room. As soon as we entered, the doors shut behind us. I ran to the door and began to bang on the door. "Let me out!" I shouted. "Please let me out!" I plead...as I kept on banging and banging. "It's no use. No one will save you," He said. I kept on banging on the door, ignoring the man. "Please, someone save me! I am begging you! "It's a waste of your energy," he said, as he inched closer to me. I felt trapped, with nowhere I can escape to. I slid my back against the door because I fear this horror will become my reality every day of my life if I don't find a way to escape. The tears burst forth like water from a dam, spilling down my face. I felt the muscles of my chin tremble like a small child. The man sat next to me, watching me cry. "Please.... not again... my body can't take it," I cried. He smiled with evil intent as he said, "But MY body can." I know it's no use to fight, but I have to! I refuse to go down without a fight. I spat in his face. "Ehh" he cried in disgust. "You little bitch!" He became distracted with wiping my saliva off his face, so I took the opportunity to kick him in where it would do the most damage. He fell to the floor groaning in pain. I hid next to the door because I knew that his men would come to see what was making their boss so distraught. When they opened the door, I took the opportunity to dash out. I kept on running through the darkened alley, not daring to look back, knowing that my life was in danger. "Get that stupid

Bitch!" The man yelled. "I will deal with her once you get her back to me!" I didn't know where I was...only that it was dark. What have I done? I was in a panic... I had to get out. "Look who I found" A man picked me up and took me to a room. This room looks like a torture chamber. My arms are chained to the wall. "You think what Derick did to you was terrible? It's not half of what I am going to do to you," He smirked. "I am sorry, I won't try that again" "It's too late," I screech in pain. "I am sorry" He laughed at me. "I warned you, but you wouldn't listen," Everything went black. I woke up chained to a bed. "You passed out from the pain" I looked beside me, and I saw him standing next to the bed. "Your pain tolerance is very low," He told me. "I hope you learned your lesson," I turn around on my aching side to not face him. I flinch in pain. "Be careful," He said. "Take the chains off her" They took the chains off me and carried me into a room that looks like a dining room.

"You must be hungry," said the man. Before shouting out the doorway, "Bring the food!" Esmeralda appeared once again, and as before, began Esmeralda appeared once again, and as before, began serving us food, regardless of whether we wanted it. She looked imploringly, clearly agitated. I ate the food. "Ask me something. I'm sure you have a lot of questions," the man said. I didn't want to talk to him, but there was nothing to say I'd get this chance again.

"Are you human traffickers? I asked. "I don't really see it as human trafficking; I see it as business," he answered.

The business of child exploitation. "Next question" "Why do you kidnap people?" "I don't kidnap people; I buy them" "How did you get me?" "You were sold to me by a guy claiming to be your grandfather. I knew it was a lie, but when I saw you, I knew I had to have you. I wasn't here when you woke; I was out taking care of matters, but at least you had a chance to meet my closest friend, Derick." Taking in everything he was saying, I found myself in something of a trance, desperately wishing that I'd never had to see either of them. With a start, I was reeled back to the here and now, and trying to compose myself, I dutifully took the bait: "What do you mean, a guy claiming to be my grandpa'?" I'm intrigued.". "All I'll say is that you've met him before, but I know for sure he is definitely not your grandpa. Any other questions?" I wanted to ask him how he could be so callous, so withdrawn from the emotions of his victims. I decided not to and continued eating my food. "I'll take that as a no. Do you want to know what I found odd?" He asked. I wanted to say no but felt I couldn't.

"Sure." "You never once asked my name." Why is that?" *I don't want to know the name of a pedophile.* "I don't know," I told him. Well, my name is Xander."

"Just great, now I know the pedophile's name," I said, covering my mouth as it dawned upon me that I had uttered these words out loud. Xander spat out his drink. His eyes widened, and he began to cough and choke. What the hell! I can't believe I just said that I thought. Well, *no going back now. I'll have to own it.* He didn't say anything upon recovering and instead kept on eating. "Do I have to call you boss, or master, or something?" "No, just Xander," he said without making eye contact.

After breakfast, he told the men to take me with the others.

"Are you okay?" Drea cried. "I am so sorry; it's my fault you got beat up." "It's not your fault," I told her as she sobbed uncontrollably into my chest, hands clutching at my t-shirt. I held her in silence, rocking her slowly as her tears soaked my chest. The poor girl really was shaken up.

Eventually, her crying stopped, and she looked up at me and asked, "Since we're friends, is it okay if I call you Maymay? Yes, Drea, you can call me Maymay," I told her. Drea and I spoke for a time, exchanging comforting words and lending one another courage, but as we spoke, I noticed that the other girls were shooting me daggers.

"Can I help you?" I asked all of them. You should be *dead,*" a girl said. "Excuse me?" Do we have a problem here?

"How are you not dead?" she went on. "Well, I am sorry to disappoint you," I said. "She's not saying she wants you dead," interjected Esmeralda. She's just pointing out that you get special treatment. "Not even Andrea gets special treatment, and she's the youngest of us all. I don't get an easy ride either, and I'm pregnant!" she said. "Trust me, I didn't ask for special treatment, if that's what *this* is, and I don't want it." Esmeralda scoffed. "Oh, believe me, you do. "I just find it so unfair that someone can get special treatment and not even appreciate it; not even *see* it." "You're acting like I can control the way Xander treats me," I said. "Oh, *Xander,* so it's first name terms, is it?" another girl said. "If I dared call him by his first name, I would probably get killed." "I'm sorry, but it's not my fault, so don't blame me," I snapped. "We're all being maltreated, and instead of all of us sticking together, you guys are getting angry at me for something I can't control." Silence. I took this as confirmation that I'd successfully made my point.

★   ★   ★

Three days passed without me seeing Xander, during which I spent most of my time with Drea. She told me about her past and where she was from Phoenix, Arizona. She was truly adorable, yet precocious, undoubtedly a result of the things that she had seen and experienced in her half-decade. We were interrupted as three men stormed into the room, and without a single word spoken, they hauled me up, followed by Andrea and Esmeralda, and led us away. Drea followed, and I made sure to keep her close had no idea what was going on, but I wanted to protect her. They bundled us into a car, and it was at this point that my mind began to race: Are *we going to Europe? Isn't it too early? Are they going to kill me?* We were driven to a large cabin where Xander and Derick were standing waiting. As I stepped out of the car, I caught a glimpse of a fresh cut under Derick's right eye. We stepped inside the cabin, and Xander pulled me aside. "You must be wondering why I had you brought here." I nodded. "I missed you," he said. Why did you bring Andrea?" I asked him, ignoring his comment. My men told me that you're fond of her, so I decided to bring her along. Esmeralda is for Derick." "Okay," I said and walked away. I didn't know what else to do. It was really quiet; no one spoke. I knew that Derick was upset about something. I could feel the tension between him and Xander. "I'm going to get some fresh air," Derick barked. "Hold up. I'll come with you," Xander said. Both men left, leaving Esmeralda and me alone. "Esmeralda, how far along come you," Xander said. Both men left, leaving Esmeralda and me alone. "Esmeralda, how far along are you?" I asked, trying to make conversation. "Nine months" "Wow, you're about pop" "Boy or Girl" "Not sure," she answered, somewhat despondently. "Maymay, can you braid my hair?" Drea asked, strolling towards us. "'Sure, Drea," I told her with a smile. I gave her Two French braids. "You look really adorable," I told her, which prompted a cute grin to grow on her face. "Malaysia, can you do me a favor?" asked Esmeralda. "What kind of favor?" "Can you cut my hair… all of it?" I studied her face, trying to ascertain whether she was alright. Her long and luscious hair? Why would she want me to cut it off? "I can, but are you sure?" I asked, making no attempt to hide my shock and confusion. "I have never been so sure about anything in my life". After searching for a while, we found a pair of kitchen scissors in a drawer -- a tad on the small side, but just about adequate. "This is your last chance. Are you sure you want to go through with? I cut her hair like she told me to and couldn't help exclaiming.

"Wow," once I'd finished. "How bad does it look? She asked. "It doesn't; you look pretty," Drea said.

"Come look for yourself," I told her, taking her hand and leading her to the bathroom. "Wow!" "I'm so relieved," Esmeralda cried. "You look beautiful," I told her.

Esmeralda smiled as she stood staring into the mirror before breaking her gaze and looking down at her stomach. "My baby is kicking. You guys want to feel it?"

We felt the baby kicking, which felt beyond wonderful."

"Thank you, Malaysia," Esmeralda smiled. At that moment, I conceded that Esmeralda was not as bad as I had thought.

"I'm sorry," Esmeralda said. "Sorry for what?" I asked.

"Sorry for being rude to you. I saw how you were getting treated, and it made me jealous because not one person has shown me any human decency," she said. "its fine, Esmeralda, I understand," I said, touching her arm. Is Derick the baby's father? I know it's not my business, but I want to know. "No, I don't know who the father is." "Sorry if that's a sensitive topic," I said. "It's fine." "What else do you want to know? I have a few questions for you too.". "How old are you?" "I'm 18" "Is this baby your first child?" "It's my third" I must've looked as stunned as I felt as she proceeded to spill the beans. "I had my first child at 11, but he died a few minutes later. I had my second child 13, but he was taken away just after turning three," She sniffled. "Maymay, I'm tired," Drea whined. "It's pretty late, Drea, let's get you to bed," I said, hoisting her up onto my back. We went to one of the rooms in the cabin, and I laid her on the bed. "Promise me you will be here when I wake up, Maymay." "I promise, Drea, now go to sleep."

I went to the living room where Esmeralda was sitting. "Do you know how Andrea was sold?" I asked her. "I heard when she used to live in the states that her foster parents staged a kidnapping to sell her," She said. "Oh...my... *God!* The people who were supposed to protect and take care of her did this to her? "I asked. "Trust me, I can relate," Esmeralda said, leaning towards me. "Can I ask you a question?"

I nodded. Her question took me by surprise. "You tried to escape already," she continued, "and seeing how protective you are of Andrea, you must have something up your sleeves. "Either way, I'm running out of time. I'm nine months pregnant, and I will not have my baby born into this mess. If we do escape, maybe I could even find my second child." she told me.

"What is your second child's name?" I asked. "His name is Andres." She told me; an expression of intense yearning plastered on her face; I took a deep breath, readying myself for the inevitable disclosure to come. "Yeah, I have been thinking of ways to escape with Drea, and now that I know you want to escape, we can come up with something together." "Let's do it NOW," she exclaimed with excitement. "Now? We don't even have a plan." Tears began to cascade down her cheeks as she spoke, "Every second I'm here, I am worried about my child; I'm terrified about bringing it into this life. It's now or never," she said, resolved. "They have weapons; we don't." "These men run a trafficking ring. I'm pretty sure they must have guns here somewhere." We went off in search of a gun, "I found one!" Esmeralda said. She pulled a revolver from under her coat. "Where did you find it?" I asked. "In Derick's stuff."

We heard the creaking sound of a door opening. "Take the gun," Esmeralda said, shoving it into my hand. I hid the gun in the back of my jeans, and once we were confident it was hidden, we headed for the front, trying desperately to act natural, stopping in our tracks as we were confronted by the sight of Derick pacing back and forth, covered in blood.

"Shit! Shit! What have I done?" he cried, just as he looked up and saw us. "What the hell happened to your hair, Esme?" "It looks hideous." "I think it looks good; short hair fits you, Esmeralda," I protested. "YOU!" Derick bellowed, pointing a trembling finger at me. "It's all your fault," he yelled. "My fault? What did I do? "Xander is *dead* because of you," he shouted. "My fault; what did I do?" "Xander is DEAD because of you," he told me. "How is that my fault? "When we were walking around, he noticed how I didn't like you, how I 'treated you,' and then the bastard threatened me. Can you believe that? He threatened me over you! Someone I saw as a brother betrayed me for you, *ugly* bitch." "Don't blame Xander's lack of loyalty towards you; I didn't ask for his help. If that was your reason to kill him, then you must've always secretly hated him." "Shut up! You're lying," he spat, practically frothing. "I have no reason to lie, and you know that deep down inside, you're relieved that he's dead." I scolded him. "Maymay, are you okay?" I heard Andrea cry. "I'm fine, Drea," I told her. "I heard yelling, and I got scared. "It's okay, Drea, go back to bed," I told her. "Andrea, come here now" "Drea, don't come here hide," I instructed her. "Shut up," He said and pulled out his gun. "If you don't come, I will kill her, and it will be YOUR fault," He told the little girl. "Drea ignores him. "As soon as I said the word Derick shot fire at the air. "I'm sorry, Maymay, I don't want you to die like my mommy and daddy," She sobbed. When the little girl came without exchanging words, Derick shot her. As much as I tried to hold it in, the pain came out like an uproar from my throat in the form of a silent scream. The beads of water started falling down one after another, without a sign of stopping. I hit the floor and tried to scream, but my voice was melted by the sound of the place. The muffled sobs wracked against my chest. The world turned into a blur, and so did all the sounds. The taste. The smell. Everything was gone. Esmeralda dragged my hand.

"Malaysia, we got to go now before he kills us too," Esmeralda muffled. He has a stupid grin on his face. "Now you know how it feels to lose someone you care about. Esmeralda flinches in pain. Without flinching, I got the revolver from the back of my pants and shot Derick over and over again. He's DEAD, Malaysia stop shooting!" Esmeralda said. "My water broke Malaysia. My baby is coming right now."

"Okay, breathe Esmeralda, breath," I told her.

I went to check on Andrea picking her body into my arms. She was faintly breathing. I don't know what to do. Andrea is life's slowing slipping away, and Esmeralda is having her baby. I held Drea's body in my arms. Why did this have to happen to this poor child? She has been through so much, and I only wanted to protect her. I wanted to be her guardian angel.

"Maymay, don't be sad now. I'm going to join my Mommy and Daddy," she faintly smiled. I kiss her on her forehead. "Rest, my little angel."

"Malaysia, I don't think I'm going to make it," Esmeralda said. I gently laid Andrea down on the floor next to me.

"Esmeralda, you need to make it; you're going to make it," I told her.

"I don't think I am Malaysia, and if I don't, please take care of my baby like it's your own promise to me that you will " Esmeralda asked. "I promise I will, Esmeralda, but you need to make it. She was moaning in so much pain.

"Deep breaths and push Esmeralda, push," I told her.

"I can see its head keep on pushing," I told her.

"It's a boy Esmeralda, you had a boy," I told her and cut his umbilical cord with the scissors I used to cut Esmeralda's hair.

Xander said.

She didn't say.

"Esmeralda! Esmeralda!" I shouted.

It was no use; she is dead. I was surrounded by dead bodies and a baby. He started to cry. I don't know what to do this poor baby has no mother because she died before she got the chance to set her eyes on him. I heard people talking, and I went to Derick's body and got his keys and wallet out of his pockets, and I got a blanket and wrapped the baby inside it. I heard the voices at the door, and I opened the window and escaped with the baby. They were outside, so I waited for them to enter the cabin.

"What happened here?" I heard one of the guys yell.

I started the car and put the baby next to me, and I put him in seat belts. I drove slowly for the baby's safety, but at the same time, I drove a little fast to get out here before anyone noticed. After I wasn't around the cabin or whatever that place was, I checked on the crying baby, and I started to cry with him, how I'm supposed to take care of the baby with no food for him to eat.

"I know, baby, you're hungry, but please sleep so I can go somewhere to find baby food," I said.

I buckled the baby in a seat belt, and I drove and saw a little market. It was a little store, and I bought baby food and water with Derick's money. I fed the baby and changed him with a t-shirt. I asked for directions for the way back in the city in French, and I asked him if there was a hotel close by. The store owner said yes and gave me directions to the closest hotel nearby. I held him and put him to sleep. This baby has gone through so much, and he doesn't even know it. I kissed him on his forehead. I know I must name him, but I don't know what to name him. I have a lot of money left over from what I took from Xander's wallet. I rented a room and asked them for baby items, but they said they didn't have any, and I should try asking other guests. I went knocking on doors with the baby on one arm. A lot of people kept on telling me that they couldn't help me. I started crying because this child needs all the help he can get. Why is the world so cruel? I went knocking on the last door for the day.

"Can you please help this poor baby and me?" I asked, looking down at the baby.

"Malaysia?" the person asked. I was stunned; it can't be that I don't do this in any way.

"Malaysia!"

The person called out my name. I didn't reply, and I was still stunned. I'm wondering how and when.

"It's me! It's really me, Malaysia," the person said. I must have stepped back because the person said, don't leave. I felt like I saw a ghost. I was trying to say words, but they weren't coming out, only tears, lots, and lots of tears.

"Your eye, are you okay?" the person asked. I was crying even harder, and this made the baby fuss.

"I'm sorry, baby," I whispered.

"Asia, whose baby's this? The person asked.

"I heard you say Malaysia," someone yelled from the room.

"Because it's her"

"Malaysia! Oh my god, Asia, I can't believe it's you."

"It's really you," I said.

CHRISTOPHER

It's Malaysia in the flesh. She looked shaken. She has bruises on her face and neck, and her shirt was covered with dried blood.

"Hi Asia," I said with a big grin on my face.

"Hello, Chris," she said back.

"Asia, I got so scared I thought we would never find you," Maysie said.

"Well, I'm here now," Malaysia said, a little preoccupied.

"Can I hold the baby?" Addy asked.

Asia was a little hesitant, but she said yes and gave Addy the baby.

"He's so cute," she said.

"What's his name?" Addison asked.

That question must have triggered her because she started crying. Maysie hugged Malaysia and tried comforting her. I don't know what to do. I have no idea what she went through, but I'm positive it wasn't good.

"I don't know, okay! I don't know," she said, crying in her sister's hands.

"His mom was supposed to name him, but she's dead, and now he's my responsibility, and I don't know anything!" she said.

"Hon, it's okay, everything alright," Maysie said.

"It's not okay. You have no idea what I've been through, Maysie," she said.

"Malaysia, maybe you need a shower and a change of clothes," Aiden said, coming out of the bathroom.

"Yah, I really need a shower," she said.

"Please watch him," She said.

"Here, hon, take this outfit and deodorant and toothbrush," Maysie said.

"Thanks"

"Don't worry about the baby; we will take good care of him," I told her.

After she went into the shower, everyone looked tense.

"What happened to her?" whispered Addison.

"She has bruises and a baby and was covered in blood," I whispered.

"Asia has been through things that we will never ever imagine," Aiden whispered.

"We need to take her and the baby to the hospital pronto," I whispered.

"Yah and that supposedly broken leg of yours," chuckled Addy.

"Laugh it up, Addy. I thought I broke my leg but guess what I didn't. It was just a sprain," I said.

"When Marcus and I went into the woods, we saw him crying and saying he was going to get eaten by a snake and that he broke his leg," Aiden laughed.

"I heard cracking noise, and I thought it was my bones, but it was the branch I slipped and sprained my ankle," I said out loud.

We heard Malaysia chuckling in the bathroom.

"Honestly, though, we need to ask whose baby's this because I know it's not hers. Right, Chris?" Aiden asked.

"I'm pretty sure you would notice if Malaysia was pregnant," I said.

"Trust me, that's not her baby Aiden," Maysie said.

"I want to know what she means. That baby is her responsibility," I said.

"The baby is my responsibility because when I helped deliver him, his mother told me that she wasn't going to make it and made me promise to take care of him as he's my own, so I have a son now," She said.

"Don't wake up the baby, please, and its okay," She said and walked into the bathroom.

"Get out now!" She yelled at me.

"Asia, let's talk, please," I said and put my hand on her shoulder. She flinched and moved away. I closed the bathroom door.

"Why are you still here? Get out now!" She yelled.

I told her.

"Asia, please talk to me?" "What happened to you?" "I just saw three people die, and I was the cause of one of their deaths," She cried on the floor.

I think she just admitted to murdering someone. I went next to her and tried to comfort her. She flinched again, but she let me touch her. I gave her a hug.

"Malaysia, I love you," I told her.

"I love you too, Chris," she said. We shared a passionate kiss. She stopped the kiss.

"Chris, we're on the floor, and I'm in a towel. I need to shower so I can get back to the baby and go out to buy him food," she said.

"Malaysia, explain to me. I'm worried, sick, and it's not just me. We all are, especially your parents," I told her.

"I saw and experienced things that I'm not ready to talk about," she said.

"Okay, when you're ready, I'm going to be here for you," I told her.

"Also, you and the baby need to go to the hospital," I told her. She didn't reply back. All she did was nod.

"Well, get out," she said.

I accidentally got a glimpse of her boobs, and it had hickeys, which were now purple. She noticed I saw them, so she pulled up her towel.

"Chris, I'm not going to shower with you in the bathroom, so please leave," she told me.

I did as I was told, and when I came out, Maysie and Addison both gave me a slap in the face.

"What was that for?" I asked.

"For not leaving when she told you too," Addy said. "We heard the shower running, and we heard Malaysia crying."

"It kills me that I can't help," Maysie said. "She's my little sister. I'm the one she's supposed to come to when she needs comforting, but I can't help her because I don't even know what she went through," Maysie cried.

"It kills me two," Aiden said. "She needs someone to open up, someone that she can feel vulnerable with without getting hurt," Aiden said.

"I can try," I said.

"Sorry, Chris, you already tried, and it didn't work," Maysie said.

"I know she doesn't want to talk to us right now, but I'm pretty sure she will open our mom," Maysie said.

"Yah but Marcus and Ray we—"

Aiden was stopped by noises in the bathroom. The noises woke up the baby, but Addy was taking care of him. I had never run so fast in my life when I ran to the bathroom door. I tried to open it, but she locked it.

"Malaysia, please open the door!" I cried while yelling, and she didn't reply.

"Asia, are you okay? Please open the door! Please!" Maysie sobbed.

"Chris, try to see if you can pick the lock, and I'll go to the front desk for an extra key," Aiden said.

"Hurry up!" I yelled.

Maysie was trying to seek her sister to open the door. Addison was trying to calm the baby while I was trying to pick the door lock open. Please be okay, Malaysia, please be okay. I couldn't pick the lock. I tried so many times, but I couldn't.

"I… got …a … extra… key," Aiden said out of breath.

I opened the door as fast as I could. I saw the shattered mirror glass on the floor. Malaysia next to it with her blood on her arms. She was crying hard.

"I just want to die! I want to be dead," she howled.

"Chris, go get something to tie her wound," Maysie ordered.

"I can't let you die, Asia. You are my baby sister, and I love you, and that's a lot of blood," Maysie said.

"How did you get to this hotel?" Maysie asked.

"I stole a car," Malaysia answered weakly.

"Where are the keys"? Maysie asked.

"In my pants pockets," She whispered.

Maysie tied her wound and put pressure on it.

"Aiden, you drive" We went to the front desk, and the lady was shocked.

Maysie was asking her for directions to the nearest hospital. We had to make a little car seat for the baby because we didn't have a car seat for him.

"Aiden, drive really fast. She's losing a lot of blood. Tears were flowing down Maysie's eyes, but she put on a brave face.

When we arrived at the hospital, they put Malaysia in surgery, and they also took the baby from us. We waited for hours for the doctor to come tell us the news. The doctor was speaking to Maysic. I couldn't understand them because I don't speak French. I tried to guess what they were saying, but I couldn't understand them, but Maysie's facial expression gave me hints of what the doctor told her. Maysie burst out crying. She was holding on to the doctor's arm, and the doctor was trying to get her off him. I managed to get her off him.

"Chris, you should get your leg checked out," said Addison.

"I'm fine," I told her.

"No, she's right, Chris, you need to get your leg checked out," Maysie said.

"What about Malaysia?" I asked.

"She's in surgery. We don't know what will happen to her, but you need to get yourself checked out," Maysie told me.

I did as I was told and got myself checked out. A few hours later, after getting X-rays on my leg, the doctor came with the results. The doctor didn't speak English, so they had to get an English translator. They told me it was just a little sprained and that I needed a leg cast and a pair of crutches. I got the leg cast and crutches and disposed of my homemade ones. I went to the waiting room to find Mrs. Johnson crying in Maysie's arms.

"My baby, my baby," She sobbed in Maysie's arms.

Mr. Johnson couldn't stay seated; he was too anxious. The doctors finally came back out and talked to Malaysia's parents. Mrs. Johnson was crying, but this time she was crying with tears of joy.

"Mrs. Johnson, what did the doctors say?" asked Aiden.

"Asia's okay, but she needs to rest," Mrs. Johnson said.

"When can we see her?" I asked."

You guys can see her tomorrow, my wife and I will stay at the hospital. You guys need to go back to the hotel. I'm pretty sure everyone is tired," Mr. Johnson spoke.

"What about the baby?" Addy asked.

"The baby is staying here too; they want to be sure he's safe," Mr. Johnson answered.

"Where did she get the baby from?" Asked Marcus.

"Her dead friend," Addy said.

"We are still unsure about what she went through while she was away, but we know for a fact she has been through so much," Maysie said.

"You guys need to check out a new room," Ray said.

We checked in our rooms, and everyone was assigned a

roommate. Maysie and Addy were together, Ray and Marcus, and Aiden and I were together.

"Chris, you need a shower," Aiden said.

I looked down and saw that I was covered with Asia's blood. I took a long cold shower. My mind was so distracted by Malaysia. I never thought she would actually try to kill herself.

"I just want to die; I just want to be dead," her words kept on repeating in my head.

"Chris, are you okay?" Aiden knocked on the bathroom door. "Sorry, man, you've been in the shower for over an hour, and I want to shower too," Aiden told me.

I got out of the bathroom so Aiden can shower too. I got ready and tried to fall asleep, but I couldn't sleep.

"Aiden, are you up?" I asked him.

"Nope, I can't sleep," he answered.

"I can't believe we almost lost her," I said.

"Yah, I am not a really big god believer because not a lot of good things have happened to me. But Malaysia living after losing that much blood was really a blessing from God," Aiden said.

"I can't believe that was the same girl we played Uno with at her house a few weeks ago," I said. "It's like a different person entered her body," I said.

"Yah, a damaged, fragile little girl who is a survivor and a warrior," Aiden said.

"Aiden, can I tell you something?" I asked.

"Come on, dude, I've been your best friend since kindergarten. No matter how pissed I'm at you, I will always be there for you. So, spill whatever you want to tell me," he said.

"I think Asia might have admitted to the murder," I whispered.

"Huh?" Dude, I can't hear you speak up," Aiden said.

"I think Asia might have admitted to the murder," I said a little louder.

"Excuse me, but where did you get this from?" he asked.

"When I was in the bathroom with her, she told me that she witnessed four deaths, and one of them was her fault," I explain.

"Chris, are you in your right mind? Malaysia is not a killer. How could you say this about her?" he asked.

"This is not a random chick. This is our friend. This was the girl who has been your girlfriend since the freshmen year of high school. This was the girl who stayed with you and was loyal even after you cheated on her. This is the girl that hosts charity events. Chris, you say a lot of stupid shit, but this shit that you just said was the dumbest shit I ever heard coming out your mouth," he said.

"You're right. I'm just tripping; it's Malaysia. She kills flies, not people" I said.

Although I know that Aiden's right, I still don't know anything that happened. She was just dropping breadcrumbs. It's so crazy how a lot can happen in such a short time. My head is pounding with frustration and curiosity. Will I ever know what happened to her?

"Chris, wake up," I heard someone call my name.

"Baby, it's me, Malaysia, your parents let me in," Malaysia said.

"Asia?" I questioned.

"Yah, your girlfriend," she said. She laid next to me, and she pecked my forehead.

"Are you feeling better?" She asked.

"No, my head is pounding," I told her. "What happened to me?" I asked.

"Babe, you got a concussion when Thomas Sinclair accidentally hit you when we were playing softball," She told me.

"That explains why my head is pounding," I told her.

The doorbell rang, and Malaysia went to go and answer it. She came back with a box of pizza, Orange Fanta, and brownies.

"I ordered pizza ahead because I thought you'd be hungry," she said.

"Have I ever told you how much I love you?" I told her.

"Yes, but you can keep saying it," She said.

"I love you; I love you so much," I told her. She had a cute grin when she heard those words.

"I love you too," she told me.

"I told my parents that I'm spending the night at Keisha's house, but guess who's house I'm actually spending the night at?" she questioned.

"Mine," I said.

"I still owe you that 80's movie marathon date," she said.

"When did you come back?" I asked.

"About a week ago, I called you and told you I loved you and that I wanted to stay with you," She said.

"Right, I remember now. I'm sorry it's my concussion," I lied. We were watching "Goonies" while eating pizza. A couple of times during the movie, I'll sneak a kiss.

"I want to do it," she said.

"Huh?"

"I want to have sex with you, Christopher," she said.

"Are you sure?" I questioned.

"I am positive, this time we'll have no distraction because your parents don't barge in your room like mine," she said. She took off her shirt and her pants.

"I can't! I can't have sex with you," I told. She tried seducing me. Although I was turned on, I couldn't have sex with her. It doesn't feel right. "Asia, I can't have sex with you, I'm sorry," I told her.

"Why can't you?" she asked.

"It doesn't feel right," I told her.

"Is it because I'm ugly?" she asked. Bruises started appearing on her body. She was crying. I tried to comfort her, but she wouldn't allow me to. Her tears were blood. She was crying blood.

"Asia, you're crying blood; we need to take you to the hospital," I told her.

"Save me, Chris! Save me. I need you to save me," She said.

"Babe, I need to take you to the hospital," I told her. She kept on crying more and more. I don't know what to do. She is crying blood on my bedroom floor. She ran away into my bathroom. I heard her crying some more. I saw blood coming out under my bathroom door. I opened my bathroom door, but I wasn't in my bathroom. I don't know where I was. It's like I was in a different universe. It's so pretty, but yet it's so weird.

"Save me, Chris! I need to be saved!" I heard Malaysia yelling. I couldn't find her. So, I followed her voice. Instead of finding Malaysia, I found us in the seventh grade, having our first kiss dancing to unwritten by Natasha Bedingfield. I heard her calling my name again, but I still didn't find her. Instead, I saw Malaysia asking me on a date in the Ninth grade in our cafeteria.

"I had a big crush on you since the seventh grade, and I never got over my feelings, although it's been two years. What I'm trying to say is that...would you go out with me?" Malaysia asked.

"Yes, I would," I told her. I saw Keisha cheering in the back excitedly for her best friend with everyone else. I kept on walking, and I saw Malaysia and me on our first date. It was awkward. I don't know who was more nervous than me or Malaysia.

"Beautiful place," she said.

"Yeah, it's," I said. I was so nervous that day my hands were very sweaty.

"Save me, Chris!" Malaysia yelled. I followed her voice, and I saw the night we had our first fight. I remembered that I got so jealous when I saw her and Thomas Sinclair in our school play kissing.

"It was my role, Chris. It meant nothing," She told me.

"Come on. Everyone knows that Thomas has a big ass crush on you!" I hollered.

"Okay, but I like you, my boyfriend. I wish you could just see that instead of being jealous," She said.

"You also said you were fine with me taking that role. Now you're behaving like a total ass hole," She said.

"I'm acting like this because I love, and I didn't like seeing you kiss another guy," I told her. She didn't say anything for a while. She just stood there, speechless. She was angry, and I could tell.

"You make me so angry," She said and walked out on me. This was also the first time I told her that I loved her. I kept on walking, and I saw the first time Malaysia was crying in my arms. She is the type of person that doesn't like it when people see her cry, so when she cried in my arms, I was so shocked. I kept on walking, and I saw the first time Malaysia told me she loved me. It was Valentine's Day, and we had a date at the restaurant we had our first date.

"This place is still just as beautiful," she said.

"Yah, it's," I told her. I was so nervous we had been dating for a while, but she still made me get butterflies. After dinner, I walked her home.

"Today was fantastic," She said.

"Today was amazing, and you look amazing," I said. We started making out, and I was about to tell her I needed to go when she said, "I love you, Chris."

"You what?" I chuckled.

"I love you," she repeated.

"I love you too," I said.

We were making out until her dad came outside and told her she needed to go inside. I remembered going home so happy that night. I kept on walking, and I found myself in Malaysia, and my one-year anniversary. We planned such a romantic day, but it didn't go as we imagined; instead, that day was a total disaster. I remembered that day ended with Malaysia, and I am making out in the rain. I also remembered catching the flu. But that day was totally worth it. We've been through so much, and I know a lot of people say that they don't believe in young love, but Malaysia Strawberry Johnson is my first love. I heard her crying again.

"Malaysia, I want to help you, but I don't know how!" I yelled. "I can't help you, Asia. I am sorry!" I yelled.

The crying stopped, and it was quiet. Way too quiet, it started raining blood. The blood was suffocating me, and I couldn't breathe.

"Dude, are you okay?" Aiden asked. It was all a dream. It was just a dream.

"Dude, you were wheezing in your dream," Aiden said.

"I was suffocating in blood," I told him. He had a question on his face.

"It's nothing, never mind," I told him.

"Well, go back to sleep. It's too early," He said.

I tried, but I couldn't sleep. So, I stayed up the rest of the night. I heard a knock on the door, and it was the girls.

"Wake up, guys," Addison said.

They brought breakfast for us.

"Chris, did you have a rough night?" Addy asked.

"He did. He woke up and told me he was suffocating in blood," Aiden said.

"That's awful. Are you okay?" Addy asked.

"I'm fine," I told her.

Marcus and Ray joined us for breakfast, and when we were finished, we went to the hospital. We were allowed to see the baby and Malaysia. I went into Malaysia's hospital room. I saw Asia holding the baby and both of her parents with her.

"Asia, you're awake," Said Maysie.

"Yah, we were discussing the name of the baby," Malaysia told us.

"Can I please talk to Malaysia alone?" I asked.

I can tell the other guys weren't happy with what I asked because they just saw Malaysia. Malaysia smiled and said yes. Everyone else except for the baby Malaysia and me.

"So, what do you want to talk about?" Malaysia asked. "I have a lot to talk about," I said. The baby started crying.

"Would you like to feed him?" She asked.

"Yah, but how do I feed him?" I asked. She giggled and said, I forgot you know nothing about babies.

"I'm an only child, so I have no idea," I said. "He's pretty adorable," I said.

"I know right," she said.

"Asia, last night, I had an insane dream," I told her.

"What was it about?"

"It was about you, about us," I told her. She had a confused look on her face, so I knew I had to explain it to her.

"I had a dream about us together in the past. Also, you were crying for help," I said.

"Me crying for your help, are you sure"?

"I don't know, I felt like you had to tell me something," I told her.

"I have nothing to talk about," she said.

"Malaysia, please, I know something terrible happened to you. I want you to know I'm here for you," I said. Tears started to flow down her eyes.

"Asia, I know it's hard to talk about it, but I want you to know I'm here for you," I told her.

You would never understand because you have never been through it. I know you mean well and it means a lot but right now I'm still in shock and I can't talk about It" she shouted. The baby started crying, and she tried to calm him.

"Please leave," she gently said. I can't do anything right. I have no clue how to talk to her. When I came out, everyone else went inside except for Addison.

"Chris, are you okay?" Addison asked.

"I'm fine," I answered.

"If you're worried about Malaysia, I want you to remember she is brave and can handle herself. She is just facing demons right now," She told me. "I might not know exactly what she's facing, but we have to be there for her. That's all we can do," Addy continued.

"I don't know how to be there for her," I whined.

"Being there for her is being there when she needs you," Addison told me.

"Come on, let's walk around," She told me.

Addy and I were walking around, laughing, and talking. She knows how to ease my mind.

"I missed our friendship," I told her.

She started laughing.

"I'm serious. Before we became more than friends, we were the best of friends,"

"Come on, Chris, you don't need to be nice to me,"

"I'm for real, Addison. You're pretty cool," I told her. She smirked and said, "You're not so shabby yourself."

Our conversation must have been so deep that I didn't even notice the wet floor caution sign. I slipped and fell on my butt. Addison was cackling really hard.

"You think this is funny?" I questioned jokingly.

"Yes, it's hilarious," she continued to laugh.

I gently tugged her so she could be near me on the wet floor. Our faces were so close to each other our breath became one. Our lips conjured, but it wasn't magical.

"I'm so sorry, I didn't mean to kiss you," I told her. She didn't say anything; she was touching her lips in shock. "It was a mistake. It meant nothing," I awkwardly babbled.

"Oh, wow, Chris!" She said and got up and left,

"I didn't mean it like that," I said. I chased after her. It's hard because I'm in crunches. "Addison, wait, I'm sorry I didn't mean it like that,"

"It's okay Chris, I understand I mean nothing to you, and I am okay with it,"

"Whoa, you're blowing things out of proportion Addy, I didn't say that," I told her.

"Just admit that's what you meant to say.

"Admit it!" She yelled.

"Fine, I admit that the kiss meant nothing to me, but that's not how I feel about you. Believe it or not, I actually care for you. You were once my best friend, and I know that things will never be the same after we slept together,"

"Remember when I told you that I had feelings for Malaysia and someone else?" She asked.

"Yah, of course, I do," I said.

"Well, that person is you," She cried. "It's funny because it feels like I'm in a love triangle, But you people don't even have feelings for me," She said.

"I'm sorry," I said.

"It's not your fault. It's mine. I can't believe that I exactly caught feelings for the boyfriend and girlfriend," she chuckled. I could tell she was hurting, but she covered it with a laugh. I had no clue on how to help, but I'll use her advice on her. "I know you're hurting right now, but I want to let you know that I'm here for you," I told her. She gave me a hug.

"Are you two together?" Marcus asked.

"It's not what it looks like," I tried to explain.

"Aren't you and my little sister together?"

"Well, not really...It's kind of complicated," I told him.

"Even if it's complicated, you thought that right now was the perfect time for you guys to have a love sac. My sister was about to die. You're so disrespectful," He said.

"Marcus, we didn't mean to be disrespectful. I was just comforting her," I told him.

"What happened...Why do you need comforting Addison?" Marcus questioned.

"Well, we kind of got into an argument.... About something private," Addison explained.

Marcus didn't look convinced; instead, he looked annoyed. "I won't mention this to Malaysia because I don't want to stir up any drama," He said and walked away.

I noticed a doctor watching us. He must have been wondering why we were making so much commotion. I went up to him.

"Hello, I'm Chris. I just want to say I am very sorry for the loud commotion," I told him.

"It's fine," He said. The man didn't sound like he was from here. Maybe he's from Spain. I went back to Addison, who seemed preoccupied.

"Are you okay, Addy?"

"I'm glad he didn't come earlier," she said.

"Yah, me too," I agreed.

Addy and I didn't say anything for a while. We just stared at one another. We decided to go to the waiting room. We saw Ray and Maysie chatting.

"Where did you and Addy go?" Aiden interrogated.

"We were walking around," I said.

He didn't say anything after that. I went to the vending machine to get myself a snack. But they didn't expect US dollars.

"Americans!" A girl behind me laughing. She is really beautiful.

"What is that supposed to mean?" I asked her.

"I mean that American tourists usually forget that American money doesn't work here" She chuckled. Maysie came to make sure that I was okay.

"Hi, my name is Genevieve" She introduced herself.

"Hi, I am Maysie. Is something wrong?" Maysie asked.

"No, I was just joking with him about American tourists thinking that the US dollars work here," Genevieve said.

"I'll pay for your snack," Genevieve offered.

"That's very sweet of you, but I'm okay," I told her.

"You allowed me to make fun of you. It's the least that I can do," she insisted.

"Alright," I caved.

"I'm going to check on Asia," Maysie said.

Genevieve and I continued to chat.

"Are you visiting someone?" She asked.

"My girlfriend is currently checked in," I told her. When I mentioned the word "girlfriend," her face changed at first, and then she went back smiling.

"Are you visiting someone?" I asked her.

"I'm looking for my brother. He's not a patient or something. He's here for police duty," she said.

"What's your brother's name?" I catechize.

"His name is Raymond," She answered.

"Why are you visiting the hospital? I mean, why didn't you wait for him at home?" I interrogated.

"Well, I don't live in this country. I live in England, and today is my last day here, so I wanted to see him before I left," She explained.

"I'm sorry," I told her.

"It's not your fault. My brother has been fanatical about this case since we lived in London, and he finally found a lead," She said. *Is this the case that her brother is obsessed with related to Malaysia?* I must have had an absent look on my face because she laughed.

"What's the case about?" I asked. I did my best to try not to sound suspicious.

"Human trafficking," she said. I felt my Jaw tense. Human trafficking, there's no way this is related to Asia. Her brother's probably some other Raymond on the police task force that is currently in the same hospital with us.

"Hu- Hu-" I tried to speak, but I'm so appalled that the words refused to come out.

"I know it sounds like something straight out of a movie, but it's actually true," Genieve said.

"I know where your brother is," I told her. I showed her where Ray was sitting.

"Gen, what are you doing here?" Ray asked his little sister.

"To see you," she answered. "I'm leaving tomorrow," She told her brother.

"I'm so sorry, Gen, I forgot," Ray said.

"I know because you're too distracted with this case," She said.

"Can I talk to you in Private Ray?" I asked.

"Sure," he said.

"Why didn't you mention that Malaysia's part of a human trafficking case!?" I lashed out.

"First off, I don't owe you an explanation, and second I told her parents who I'm supposed to tell," he said in a calm but spiteful voice. "I honestly don't see why you care, weren't you kissing that Addy girl?"

"You saw it!"

"Yah, I saw, don't worry, I didn't say anything because it's none of my business," He said.

"Do you have any leads to who might have sold her?" I asked.

He looked annoyed and said, "I don't owe you any explanation."

"I know that, but can you please tell me?" I asked.

"No," He said and walked away.

Damn Malaysia, what did you go through? If I can't get through to Ray, maybe Maysie could. I think he might be attractive to her. I went to Maysie and elucidated to her what happened. She marched straight to Raymond.

"How could you not tell us?" She roared.

"You told her," Ray rolled his eyes.

"Because I didn't need to tell you," He said.

"I'm her sister!" Maysie yelled.

"You're not her parent or guardian,"

"What if something happens to your little sister, and you had no clue about what happened to her, but you knew the person that had information on what happened? How would you feel?" she asked.

"It already happened to me, but I found the information on my own,"

"You understand my pain, so why did you make me go through that?" she said.

"I was simply doing my job," He said. Addy and Marcus came together.

"Marcus, there's something I need to tell you," Said Maysie. She explained to him.

"How could you? I thought we were cool," Marcus spoke.

"We are cool. It is just that it's my responsibility to tell the parent or guardian," Ray said. With that, Marcus jumped on Ray and punched him in the face.

"Marcus! Marcus, stop!" Maysie yelled. She tried pulling Marcus off of Ray. The rest of us joined.

"Marcus, what is wrong with you?" Maysie questioned.

"He knew May. He knew what happened to Asia," he said.

"I told your parents that I have suspicions that she might have been kidnapped and sold into human trafficking to be a sex slave," Ray said. "I wasn't trying to worry you because it was just suspicion," He told Marcus.

"Just tell us everything you know," I said.

"What are you guys doing here?" Aiden asked. I told him everything, and he had the same reaction as Marcus.

"Why is everyone trying to beat me up?" Ray asked. No one answered because he knew the answer to his own question. Ray clarified everything to us. He didn't really know much about Malaysia's case.

"Ray, I'm sorry, I shouldn't even be mad at you. I should've been mad at my parents for not telling us what happened," Marcus said.

Marcus walked away from us. I could tell that he was frustrated. We all are. Now we know what might have happened to Asia. But how did she escape? I heard they have strict security. I could tell she went down without a fight, look at how bruised she is. Maysie followed Marcus, and I followed her. Marcus started talking to his parents. I joined their family conversation.

"Bro, go sit down. This is for family only," He said.

"I might not be a part of your family doesn't mean I don't care for Malaysia. I have every right to be in this conversation," I preached.

"I thought you and Asia's relationship was complicated," He said.

"It's, but that doesn't mean I don't care for your sister," I admitted.

Marcus was irritated with me. I could tell, but he ignored me because he had bigger fish to fry, which is his parents.

"Mom, Dad, this is the second time you left me in the dark about, and honestly, I am tired of it," he said.

"Let not talk near here Asia might hear you let," Mr. Johnson said.

We walked away near Asia's hospital door and went a little farther.

"We were going to tell you guys we just had a lot on our minds. The number one thing was finding your sister. When you guys found her, we were worried if she was going to be okay," Mrs. Johnson said.

"That's not an excuse for not telling us. We are all worried about Asia," Maysie calmly stated.

"You're right, honey, we should have told you guys," Mrs. Johnson said.

"We're sorry for not mentioning it to you earlier," Mr. Johnson said.

Mrs. Johnson added, "We're also so sorry that you guys had to find out like this."

"As long as you promise no more secrets," Marcus said.

"We promise," Mr. and Mrs. Johnson said at the same time.

Have you guys talked with Malaysia yet?" I asked.

"No, we haven't. We are not trying to scare her," Mr. Johnson said.

"Speaking of that, I would if you stop trying to force my daughter to talk about the issue that happened to her. She's clearly not trying to talk to right now," Mr. Johnson barked.

"She's sensitive right now. Whenever she's ready to talk, she will talk," Mrs. Johnson spoke.

I told them that I wouldn't and that I wanted to apologize to Asia. They allowed me. I walked to the hospital room to see an empty room. Malaysia and the baby were gone. I ran to the Johnsons. It's extremely because, for the second time today, I had to run with crutches and a cast.

"She's gone," I said out of breath.

"She and the baby are gone!" I screamed.

MALAYSIA

I walked around in the hospital carrying the baby. Carrying the baby is harder than I thought. The wound covered with bandages, where I stabbed myself on my stomach, is extremely painful. I know I'm supposed to rest, but I couldn't stand staying in that hospital room any longer. I got tired of waking up with the hospital blinding lights down my face with my parents sitting on the chairs across from me. My parents refuse to let me out of their sight because they're afraid of me trying to kill myself again. So, when they left the room, I saw it as an opportunity to explore the hospital halls. I couldn't leave the baby alone, so I decided to bring him. I kind of regret it because I'm in pain, and the hospital smell is making me nauseous. The hospital smells like sick people and sanitizer. I looked down, and I was bleeding. My tomato red blood dripped down my hospital gown. I strained myself too much. I know I'm supposed to be resting until my stitches heal. But I couldn't. I had to get out of the hospital room, and I was feeling claustrophobic. The pain I'm feeling is insane.

"Malaysia!" I heard someone called. I looked up Addison.

"Oh shit, you're bleeding!" she yelled.

Really, I didn't notice," I said in a sarcastic tone.

She took the baby and walked me back to my hospital room, and called the nurse. The nurse got mad and told me I'm supposed to relax. I apologized. I had to get my stitches redone. I asked the nurse not to tell my parents, but she told me she had to. After I got my stitches redone, my parents were nagging me about relaxing. They weren't mad at me, just worried. I remember after my surgery, I was in some kind of a trance. I felt like I was sleeping, but I was awake with my eyes closed. I couldn't open them or move my body. I thought I was about to die. I heard my parents crying over me. I've never heard my dad cry, so when I did, I was stunned. But at the same time, I was in disbelief because I felt like I was in a trance. Addison came to check on me. My mom didn't want to leave because she knows about Addison and I is beef. I gave her a slight nod to let her know it was okay. After my parents left, it was really weird.

"You are keeping him,"

"Yeah,"

"He's adorable."

"Thank you," I smiled.

"I'm glad you're doing much better" "Thanks, but I'm still in pain,"

"You still haven't come up with a baby name?" she asked.

"No, we're still deciding on the name," I told her. We didn't say anything for a few minutes. I was trying to tell her to get out without exactly saying anything. She didn't take the hint. Instead, she told me a lame joke that was kind of funny.

"I'm so glad you're okay,"

"Thanks," "Addison, I am grateful that you helped me, but what are you doing here?" I asked.

"To check on you," she answered.

"I meant, what are you doing in Africa?" If she and Chris are together, I would be happy for them. I'll be a little stung because if they are, then He moved on so quickly. Unless they were in a relationship while we were dating. No, this can't be. I'm worrying, and even if they did, it's not my problem anymore.

We are not together. Then why was he okay with the kiss? Did he cheat on her with me?

"Malaysia!" Addy called my name.

"Yes," I said.

"The reason why I came here was for you,"

"For me?"

"Believe it or not, I care about you,"

I couldn't help but laugh. I laughed so hard that my stitches started to hurt.

"Addy, we haven't been friends for like five years," I told her.

"But I still care for you," she said.

I continued to laugh. Is she on crack or something? Maybe she has dementia or something. She slept with my boyfriend. That is something I would ever do to her.

"I know we had issues in the past, Asia, but I really do care for you," "We have problems because you created those problems."

She didn't say anything, she was just quiet, and she looked at the ceiling.

"I'm sorry"

I was in a daze, which I couldn't think or speak clearly. Addison Miller, apologize! Who would've thought?

"I know me saying sorry is not enough, but I'm truly am,"

"A few weeks ago, you tried to sleep with my ex," "Ex?"

"Chris didn't tell you I dumped him, again?" No, he didn't" "I know that a few weeks ago, I was trying to have sex with your ex, but you wouldn't understand," You're right. I can't understand because I don't do that," "You are such bitch" she said.

"At least I don't pretend to be a victim,"

"When have I ever pretended I was the victim?" she asked.

"When you started copying me, I asked you nicely to stop, but instead, you acted like we hated you. When I only told you to stop copying me because it was annoying. Not only that, during freshmen, Keisha and I tried to befriend you again, but you didn't want to. Which was fine with us, but you had the audacity to act like you were better than us and kept on telling people we were bitches to you," I told her.

"You wouldn't get it," she said.

"Excuses"

"You don't understand me. You never will." "You are right. I don't, just like I don't understand you coming all the way to Africa,"

"Did you come to win over Chris?" I inquired.

"Is that what you think about me?"

"Yah, I do," "I came all the way here, and you think I did it for Chris?"

"Yah, I know you didn't do it for me," I told her.

"Wow!" she yelled.

"It's true. You are so obsessed with Chris. I'm going to be honest with you, Addy. It's sad and creepy," I told her. She started crying. The bitch really started crying.

"Boohoo, I hurt your feelings," I said. "I hate you," Addy said.

"I know, sweetheart,"

"You know what? I'm not mad at you," I told her. Addy was sobbing.

"It's Chris who cheated on me, he could've cheated on me with anyone, but he cheated on me with you," I said. "I was never mad at you, Addison. I never hated you when I found out; I was just disappointed". Addy was still whimpering, but this time she was looking at me. "I know you slept with him because you hated me. I don't know what I ever did to you," "You only went after Chris because I liked him, and I don't know if you caught feeling for him during that process or what" "Have I ever wrong you?" I asked. I looked at her in astonishingly crystalline eyes.

"No," she softly answered. I didn't look away; I kept on staring at her. I need to understand her.

"Then why do you hate me so much?!" I call out.

"I know I said I hate you, but I really don't. I hate myself".

"I hate myself," her tears burst down her face like a dam. She got up from where she was sitting and sat on the side of my bed. "You're right. I never liked Chris. I was just jealous of you guy's relationship," She admitted. "But that was at first. Then I caught feelings for him when he and I were best friends. I didn't care that you guys were in a relationship. I wanted him because I knew I couldn't have the person that I loved," she said. "We only had sex once, and he felt so guilty, I knew I lost him after that. I wasn't that upset that I lost him. I was upset that I lost you even though I never had you," she softly spoke.

"Me?" My stomach twisted and my skin tingly.

"You."

I don't know how to respond. What do I say? I chose not to say a word.

"I have loved you since seventh grade. You never noticed because you were too busy gawking at Chris". "I knew you guys were meant for each other, you could just tell. After you two broke up, both of you guys' sparks went away," she explained.

"I was heartbroken, Addy! Heartbroken, you might not know how it feels".

"I am the definition of heartbroken. I live it every day. I wake knowing that you will never love me". "I've cried myself to sleep because of you. I really never understood why him? And I still don't understand why you love him when he easily cheated on you when you could love me, and I would be so loyal and treat you way better than he does" "I wanted to make you feel how I felt," she said

"Excuse me?"

"I wanted you to feel how I feel, heartbroken and alone," she cried.

"You're pathetic,"

"Only for you," she giggled.

I jumped a little. Her laugh frightened me. She is crying and laughing at the same time with mascara dripping down her face.

"You did that for me to understand your pain, and you expect me to love you back, Addy."

"You don't love me, Addy. You're just obsessed with me. I think you have obsessive love disorder," I told her.

"My love for you is not a disorder," she said while playing with my hair.

I'm so petrified that I became stiff, I tried to move my body, but I couldn't. She inched closer to my face; I could smell her expensive perfume. She kissed me, her lips were soft like velvet, and it tasted like cherry Chap Stick.

"I love you," she whispers. "I am so sorry, Addy, I am not into girls".

"I've always dreamt of our first kiss Malaysia. It was supposed to be magical" "Why couldn't at least let me have that?" she demanded.

"I'm sorry, I just didn't want to lead you on"

"You're my dream girl," she said. I could hear the hurt in her voice. She is devastated. "The only thing I've ever long for five years is for you to love me back" "You and Chris don't love me," she said. "I wish you could see that I could treat you like a queen, I wish you could see that all I want is the best for us, and I wish you could see how much you mean to me, I wish you could see!" "Malaysia, I only wish you could see what I see," she told me. "I won't force my love on you anymore. I now know you are incapable of loving me back" "I can try to move on, but you will always be my first love. Maybe someday I can look back and laugh at this moment," Addy said. "Once again, I'm sorry for everything, Asia,"

"There are baby wipes in the baby's bag. You can wipe your face," I told her.

"Thanks," she said. "I can't believe the baby didn't wake up. We were so loud," she said.

"Because he's a good boy," I said.

"What are you going to name him?" She asked.

"I don't know," I said.

"Can I ask you a question, Asia? She asked while wiping her face with the wipes.

"Feel free to ask," I told her.

"What did you go through?"

"I saw, thinks Addy, and I am not trying to be rude or anything, but you're not the one I want to tell what I went through," I said.

"You must have gone through hell, but I want you to see that this little boy was the good that came out of it," she told me. Everything I went through feels like a movie that I couldn't stop. It was happening in front of me, and I couldn't do anything.

"Yah, that's why I'm keeping him"

"He is so cute"

"Thanks," I said. Our conversation went back to the way it started dry and awkward.

"How do I look?" she asked.

"You look pretty," I told her. "Addy, I want to let you know I appreciate you coming all this way just for me. I know I sounded ungrateful, but I just thought you came here for Chris," I said.

"I would do anything for you, Asia"

"Alright, I'm going to join the others," she said and left.

"Goodbye," I said. My parents came inside as soon as Addison walked out.

"Are you okay?" My mom asked.

"I'm fine," "Baby are you sure?"

"Sweetheart, you don't look so good," my dad told me.

"I'm good. I'm just really exhausted," I said.

"Maymay!" I heard someone call me.

"Drea! Drea! Drea!" I called out she was lying on the floor shivering.

"I missed you," I told her.

"I don't want to die, Maymay," Drea cried in my arms.

"Why did you fail me?" Andrea moaned.

"Don't fail my child like you did to me," Esmeralda said.

"Take care of my baby boy Mateo."

"I'm so sorry, guys," I sobbed. "I failed you," I cried.

"Malaysia!"

"Go get the doctor, Dwayne," My mom called my dad.

"Esmeralda! Andrea!" I squall. "I'm so sorry I failed you. I'm sorry that I couldn't protect you!"

"Baby, its okay," My mom said.

She gave me a hug, and I bawled in her arms.

"My baby!" my mom cried.

I couldn't help it; my tears were just bursting out. The doctor came and checked on me. I told her that I had a nightmare. The nightmare felt so real it felt like I was living it. My dad gave me a hug and kissed my forehead.

"Asia, we want you to let us know what happened to you," My dad said.

"Who are Esmeralda and Andrea, and how did you fail them?" My mom asked.

My throat tightened, my chin trembled, and I let out gut-wrenching sobs that tore through my chest. I let out the ugliest cry. Thinking about them breaks my heart each time.

"Esmeralda is the baby's mother, and Andrea is a little girl that I met," The words couldn't come out without me sobbing.

"We are so sorry, sweetheart," my dad said.

My headaches from crying so much.

"It's okay, sweetheart, if you're not ready to share, we won't force you," my dad said.

I was still in my momma's arms. She didn't want to let go of me. I was in her arms until I fell asleep. I feel like my momma feels like she failed me, just like I feel I failed Esmeralda and Andrea. Tears rolled down her cheeks and fell on my hair. I fell asleep in my momma's arms like a baby. When I woke up, my parents were sleeping on the seats next to me. I had to use the restroom, so I walked to the bathroom. I turned on the lights and looked at my reflection. I look horrendous. My face was still swelling and bruised my neck purple. My eyes turned purple from nurses. It looks like I got trampled by elephants. I dropped down on the floor, crying. My bruised ribs hurt from me screeching. My mom came into the bathroom and saw me on the floor.

"What's wrong, honey?" she questioned.

"I'm hideous, momma!" I yelled.

Never in my entire life have I yelled at my mom. But the pain that was feeling had to be expressed.

"No, baby, you're so beautiful," she said.

"No, I'm not, momma! Look at me!" I squall.

"We will get the people that did this to you," She spoke.

"Impossible," I spoke softly.

"Asia, there is something that I need to tell you," My momma said.

"You guys were the ones that sold me," I said. I moved away from her just to be safe.

"No! I would never sell you!" She said. "You are my baby. I birth you. I can never do that to you," she said.

"If it's not that, then what did you want to tell?" I demand.

"Officer Smith told us that you might have gotten involve in human trafficking," Explained my momma.

"Might? I was involved in human trafficking."

"I had a rape test done on you. Your sister told me that you never took a shower because you tried to commit suicide."

"It came out positive," she cried. "I am so sorry, baby, I am so sorry," She sobbed. "I'm supposed to protect you, and I couldn't even do that. We did look for you put prize money for you, but no one found you,"

"Momma, if I didn't escape, I don't think you would have ever seen me again."

"Baby, please tell me what happened to you."

"I'll try to explain to you without getting emotional," I told her. "I somehow got sold into human trafficking. I met a little girl.

She was only five, momma. Only five, which broke my heart, she told me her name was Andrea, and I nicknamed her Drea. Then I met the baby's mother. Her name was Esmeralda. She was only a couple of years older than me. There are a lot of kids, boys, and girls, but the leader put me in a room filled with only girls. I'll start from the beginning, so I don't get you confused."

"Okay," she said and patiently listened.

"When I got sold, I was woken up with chains on arms, which suffocated me. A guy named Derrick came to check on me, but I kicked him in the balls and tried to escape. They caught me, and he bit the crap out of me. I passed out. The boss came as chained up he took to his private room where Esmeralda. Things happened to me in that room that I wish I could forget. My mom is listening to everything that I said without interrupting me.

After he was done, they took me to the other girls. I saw girls of all ages and different races, but the smallest one was Drea. She caught me by surprise. I wanted to be there for her as soon as I saw her. A man tried to take Drea. Fortunately, I was able to stop him; however, I couldn't protect myself. He took me to a room when I heard the men talk about the business they were planning on doing around the world. After that, I was told to go back to Xander's room, and I fought him harder this time, but I wasn't left on the hook. Momma he- he- he -"

"You don't have to say it, baby. I can tell that it hurts," she said in a soothing tone.

"That happened, and in the morning, we had breakfast together. They worship him like he is a king. He told me that I could ask him questions, and I must have been really curious. I asked him who sold me. He told me, a guy pretending to be my grandpa," I said.

My mom gasped and said, "That can't be."

"They took me back to the other girls after we were done eating breakfast. Some of the other girls became angry at me because Xander was giving a special treat, and he allowed me to call him by his first name. Three days later, the man came and got Esmeralda, Drea, and I. I was terrified I thought I was going to die. Instead, they took us to a cabin. Where we met Xander and Derick. The two men went away, and the girls and I stayed in the cabin. This is when I had the chance to know Esmeralda better. She was 18 Momma, just a couple of years older than me. She told me that this child was her third child Momma. I also learned that Drea might have been set up by her foster parents. Esmeralda asked me to cut her hair, which I did. Esmeralda and I discussed how we were going to escape and when searched for weapons and she found a gun in Derick is things. She gave me the gun when heard the door. What we saw at the door was unexpected. Derick was covered in blood and was panicking, and Xander was nowhere to be found. He blamed me for him killing Xander. I told him that he always wanted him dead; that's why he killed him. He called little Andrea out; I instructed her to go in the room and hide. Derick threatened to kill me, so she came and out to protect me. But he–he-he-he –Drea!" I whimpered. "Everything happened so fast the next thing I noticed was that I kept on shooting at him and he went to the ground. Momma, I'm a killer," I said.

"It wasn't your fault," I heard my dad call from outside the door.

It hurts every time I think about it, and the tears fill my eyes. My mom gave me a hug and told me that this must be really hard for me to talk about. This topic is not easy at all for me to talk about, and whenever I think about, I become emotional.

"It wasn't your fault," I heard my dad call from outside the door.

"May I come in? He asked.

"Yes, you may," I answered.

"Baby, it's really not your fault he would've killed you like he killed his friend and that little girl," My dad said. "I promise you did the right thing. You protected yourself," he went on.

"It's a weight that I will forever have," I told him.

They didn't say anything because it's the truth. My mom just held me tighter.

"After I shot him, Esmeralda is water broke, so I had to deliver the baby. There was so much blood everywhere I cut the baby umbilical cord with scissors. Esmeralda asked me to watch her baby. She told me she was going to die. After I delivered her baby, she died, and I heard people at the door. I took Derick's wallet and keys to the jeep. That's how I was able to get to the hotel and rent a room," I told them.

"Malaysia, you are a survivor," my mom said.

I am a survivor. I am a fighter. I can tell my parents wanted to cry, but they wanted to be strong for me. Later on that day, my parents asked me to talk to the officer. I told the officer everything that had happened to me for the past weeks. He told me that I was incredibly lucky to escape. He said only a few could do that. I know that was supposed to help me feel better, but instead, it made me feel awful. The others deserve freedom way more than I do. I don't deserve this at all. The officer also asked me if I communicate with anyone strange. I told him I don't remember, but he and my parents stepped outside the hospital to talk. I'm quite sure everyone knows what happened to me by now.

Maysie and Marcus came into my room to check on me. They both laid on my bed, and I was in the middle, which made me feel like I was stuck in a sandwich. They both didn't speak. I really appreciated that I like their presence, although none of us were talking to each other. We used to do this all the time when we were young when one would feel down. My siblings are truly the best. I couldn't have asked for a better brother or sister. We laid in there until Marcus talked. He is always the first one to talk.

"Did you come up with the baby's name, if not? You can name him after me, the best uncle ever," Marcus Joked.

"I actually thought of a name for him," I said.

"Really! What?" Asked Maysie.

"Please let that name be Marcus," Marcus said.

"No, it's not Marcus," I said. "His name will be Mateo," I told them.

"I still think Marcus is way better, but Whatever Asia," Marcus joked.

"Fine, his middle will be Marcus," I said. Marcus burst with joy, which was really annoying, but in an adorable way.

"Why, Mateo?"

"I had a dream, and his mother named him Mateo,"

"Mateo Marcus Johnson," Marcus said.

"Our family loves names that start with M," Maysie laughed. We heard a knock on the door, and it was Aiden.

"Hi, Aiden," I said. I never really had a chance to talk to Aiden as much as I talked to the others. He came and gave me a hug while crying in my arms.

"I'm so sorry,"

"What are you sorry about?" "For not being there for you," He said.

"Aiden, you being here means the whole world to me," I said. Then Chris came in, and everyone left the room.

"I'm sorry, Malaysia," He said. "Malaysia, I'm so sorry!" Chris exclaimed. "I love you so much," he went on. "You are my first love and the love of my life," He cried.

I don't want to cry. I'm tired of crying. However, complete hopelessness converted into tears that rain down my face at lightning speed. He wiped my tears away, and I looked up at him. I saw his red and swollen eyes as his eyes filled with hot tears, and his chin trembled. My headaches from me crying so much. I'm tired of crying. I hate crying; I just want to stop crying. Moans escape my lips as a suppressed sound of hiccups.

"I love you so much," He cried. "You are the best thing that ever happened to me, and I'm so sorry. I thought I was never going to see you again," he told me.

"I love you too," I cried. "I love you so much, Chris," I told him. "When I was there, all I was thinking about was you guys," I said. "I know I was rude, but I'm just so angry, and I took it out on you," I said. "You came all this way for me, and I was a bitch, plus seeing Addy made me jealous," I said

"She came here for you,".

"I know, she and I talked, and she opened up to me,"

We didn't say anything, the place was quiet, but it is not the awkward quiet. I looked at him in his alarmingly vacant eyes, and I couldn't help but smile a little. He came all the way here for me. He looked for me, he says he loves me. I love him so much. I look so terrible, and he's still here.

"You're so beautiful," he said and kissed my forehead.

"No, I'm not. Look at me," I said.

"Don't ever say that you're stunning," He said. I gave him a hug. It feels so good to be wrapped around his arms. He smells so good, like pine and expensive cologne. He smells rich, and he is rich. "I will always be here for you," He whispers in my left ear.

A lot of people might say that I'm way too young to know what love is, but I know in my heart that I love Chris, and he will always be my first love.

"Marry me?" he asked.

"You are joking, right?" I questioned.

"I'm half-joking, and I'm half-serious," He said.

"Chris, I'm sixteen, and you are seventeen," I said.

"Your parents got married at a young age," he spoke.

"But we are not my parents," I said. "I can't do all that right now, Chris. I need time to heal," I said.

"I know I will never truly be healed or anything, but marriage at a young age is something I'm not ready for," I said. "I'm sorry," I said.

"It's okay, I'll just wait until we are old, but you will be my wife," he said and smiled at me.

He gave me a kiss on my forehead. I now know he was meant for me.

A few weeks later

It feels like I've been in this hospital for centuries, and today Mateo and I get to finally check out. I've grown to love him so much that everyone started saying that I'm overprotective over him. Tomorrow we are going back to California, but before I go, I told my parents that I wanted to set candles for Andrea and Esmeralda. Aiden, Chris, and Addy already went back to the states because school started.

"How are you feeling, baby?" My mom asked.

"I'm ready to leave. I really hate hospitals," I said.

"I know, baby, it will get better now," "Look at what I saw at the store for Mateo," My sister said.

"It's so cute. He will look so adorable in it," "You sound like such a mom. It's scary," Marcus said.

"There is nothing wrong with sounding like a mom," My momma said.

"Yah, nothing wrong with it," I said.

"I wonder how Koko is going to feel about Mateo," Maysie said.

"She is going to love him"

"Well right now she is going to be angry, you guys left her at a dog hotel and then brought a baby," Marcus said.

I'm sure Koko will Mateo, hopefully she does.

I picked up Mateo. He is so cute and adorable. I can't wait for us to go to California. We are going to go baby shopping and buy him the cutest things ever. He is my little man, my heart. We checked into our hotel room. I'm so happy that I don't have to be in that hospital anymore. I was getting sick and tired of it. I took a shower while my parents watched over Mateo.

I'm so grateful for my parents instead telling me that I can't keep Mateo because he's not my baby that supported me and said they would get me a lawyer for Mateo staying in the states and me keeping him.

After I was done, I got Mateo ready with the outfit that Maysie bought for him. He is wearing a grey short sleeve that says Auntie's bestie with a dark blue overall. He looks so cute, and I did his curly hair. He has emerald eyes just like his mom. We went to buy candles and balloons for Mateo's mother and Andrea. We found a beautiful place to put those things. Mateo is chilling in his car seat, not knowing that we are saying goodbye to his birth mother. My parents at our side, I was crying in their arms. They gave me a hug, and we let the balloons go.

"Can you guys please leave us alone?" I asked my parents.

"Okay, we will be in the car if you need us, sweetheart," My dad said.

They left, and it was only Mateo and me.

"I'm so sorry, Andrea! I'm sorry, Esmeralda!" I called out loud. "Esmeralda, I named your baby Mateo. I had a dream that is what you wanted to name him," I said. "I promise you that I'll take very good care of him," I cried. "I won't let anything happen to him, and I'll love him like my own," I sobbed. "As for you, Drea, I hope you meet your mom and dad," I said. "This world didn't deserve you, and I hope that wherever you go, it's way better. Baby, you deserve so much better you didn't deserve to go through this, especially since you are just a baby," I told her. "I just hope you guys rest easy and peaceful. You guys didn't deserve this hate that the world gave," I told you. "I'm so sorry," I said. I fell on my knees, and my shoulder fell. It was so terrible that the world has come to this.

"Well, Well, well," I heard a voice say.

"It's the bitch that tried to kill my brother" I heard her voice before it sounded so familiar.

I turned around, and I saw the girl! She has bright red long hair that reaches all the way to her butt and pale skin.

"You're actually pretty. I can see why he was obsessed with you," She said.

"Take the baby and her," she said.

"Momma! Daddy!" I yelled. "Help! Help! Somebody helps us!" I shouted from the top of my lungs that it burns.

"Shut her up right now," The pale girl said. The next thing I know, a buff arm was around my neck. He put a napkin on my mouth that made me feel dizzy.

"Hel—"

"You are going to sleep. By the time you wake up, you won't know where you are," said the bright red hair lady.